MURDER ON BOSTON COMMON
MASSACHUSETTS COZY MYSTERY

ANDREA KRESS

Chapter 1

1933

AMANDA BURNSIDE SAT at the breakfast table in the morning room of her Beacon Hill home pushing the fluffy scrambled eggs idly around her plate. She briefly wondered if she could possibly move them into position to spell 'bored,' the emotion that she was experiencing as she looked at the tiny flowers that decorated the dish.

Looking up, she saw her younger sister, Louisa, energized for whatever her day would bring, which had to be more interesting than what awaited Amanda. Another day as a volunteer doing paperwork for the Children's Indigent Clinic. Pushing records around the surface of a scarred desk in a small room on the administrative floor of the main hospital, doing good works but not feeling particularly enthusiastic about it.

Most of her friends were in the same boat: ex-debutantes from wealthy families who divided their day between volunteer work, shopping, social activities and waiting to be married. Amanda had been successful at all those things except the getting engaged part, and it wasn't for lack of interest from her male acquaintances. The problem was, she enjoyed being single and independent and knew once a ring was on her finger, she might feel confined to the more complicated responsibilities of life. Not just yet, she thought.

Her current situation had become stale, and she was looking for a change. So was Fred Browne, the young doctor whom she had been seeing for some time. *A lovely man* is how she thought of him. Kind, attentive, respected by her family. And itching to get married. She could see it in his eyes and was flattered, but sadly she felt no spark of passion or excitement toward him.

"You are going to mash those poor eggs that Cook works so hard to make light," Louisa said.

Her sister looked up from beneath her lashes with disdain. "That can't be the only thing on your mind. You're in too good of a mood for this dreary January day."

"The sun will come out at some point," Louisa responded, wiping her mouth on a napkin and getting up. She glanced at the dainty watch on her wrist. "I'd better be going soon."

Amanda put her elbow on the table and sank her head into her hand, a posture her parents would never have permitted, but her mother was busy organizing the household for the day and her father had already gone to his law office. With little enthusiasm, she hoisted herself out of the chair and tried to put on a happy face before tackling the day.

Little did she know an interesting development was to come her way.

It was a short ride to the hospital and Amanda had the luxury of her own car, which made the commute more pleasant than having to take public transport, something Louisa said she had come to enjoy for the variety of people she encountered. But then her sister was taking classes in social work, a reputable pursuit for someone who would become a society matron, and because of that, she considered any opportunity to observe the working class as part of the curriculum. What a change from the somewhat timid girl of the previous year.

Amanda was clear of most of the rush hour traffic and pulled into the parking lot behind the hospital, glancing over at the Indigent Children's Clinic's sad building. It looked as if it were built in haste and not too sturdily some years back, as if poor families were expected to be a thing of the past one day. If anything, Boston grew larger because of the people moving in from farms due to the Depression and immigrants attracted to the constant building and commerce. Most of them came with great hopes, tremendous energy, but not much money.

The building was undergoing renovation, previously having been a warehouse with high ceilings where all the warm air drifted upward, leaving the rooms below cold and drafty. Rooms, if you could call them that. They were basically partitions that delineated one exam area from another with no ceiling to speak of, affording little privacy and incessant noise. The renovation was intended to solve some of those issues and the work crew had probably been on site for a few hours already, bundled against the cold as they worked, a large trash can with a fire going to provide a bit of warmth for cold hands as needed. Some protection from the wind was provided by a galvanized metal shed that had been installed nearby and they huddled close by.

Mercy Hospital had a relatively new Executive Director, Pierce Barlow, a full-time administrator rather than just Chair of the Board, the first non-physician to lead the organization. The Board had made a bold choice after lengthy debate and decided that what the hospital needed was someone who could manage staff, a sizeable budget, make sure the regulatory requirements were met and hopefully ingratiate himself with the wealthy residents of the city to raise funds that were always needed to serve the populace.

Amanda took the elevator to the tenth floor and saw the familiar face of Miss Bailey stationed behind her desk, ready to greet visitors. The previous year there had been what appeared to be a break-in and the police had recommended better security. Part of that was an office for Miss Bailey, which hadn't happened yet, and restricted access to the administrative floor, also not yet accomplished. The new Executive Director was made aware of the previous incident and had already drawn up plans to correct the situation.

Remembering it, Amanda wondered what had become of Detective Halloran, the intriguing Irish policeman who had worked to unravel the mystery behind that break-in. He was very handsome, sure of himself and not in the least intimidated by what her mother would refer to as 'his betters.' She smiled at the antiquated language her mother sometimes used as if they lived in Victorian times. But that was still the habit of the upper class in Boston, whom the local folks referred to as the Boston Brahmins, with equal respect and derision.

"Morning, Miss Burnside," Miss Bailey said with her usual cheery smile. She had the knack of always being dressed in the latest fashion, though how she could afford it, Amanda had no idea. Perhaps she was one of those handy girls who pored over magazines and gazed in shop windows and could create an imitation frock in an evening. If so, she was successful and always looked sharp.

"Mr. Barlow would like to see you if you have a minute," she said, pausing the incessant typing that seemed to occupy most of her day.

Amanda went down the short hallway to the room where she did the paperwork and plopped her coat onto the rack in the corner after taking off her hat, scarf and gloves. Winter was such an annoyance, she thought. Her mother's family were old Yankees who had made their wealth in the days of whaling, and they were frugal in expending it. While some of Amanda's friends wintered in Florida, her family thought that was frivolous. One didn't do that. One went to the family's beach house in Maine in the summer where the temperature was often as cold as Boston in winter, the mosquitoes were a plague, and a swim in the icy Atlantic was considered character building.

Betsy, one of the fellow volunteers, would probably come in about eleven o'clock and then take her long lunch break at twelve-thirty. Sometimes that was the extent of the hours she put in twice a week, the excuse being that since she was engaged, she had so much planning to do for the wedding. Amanda was always startled by that comment since she recalled that it was to take place in May, surely more than enough time to get everything in order.

She tapped on the side of the open door to Mr. Barlow's office, pleased that, unlike the former occupant. he welcomed impromptu visits from staff although she was not strictly an employee.

"Miss Burnside, how nice to see you this morning. I am always impressed by how, even in your volunteer capacity, you keep to your assigned hours."

"Thank you," she replied, sitting down after he motioned her to a chair that faced the glass-topped desk.

"You did some work down at the Clinic, I was told. What do you think of the plans for improvement?"

"They were certainly needed. Do you know when they are expected to be completed?"

"Later than I would like," he said. Everything was on a large scale with this man, his height, his shoulders, his hands, his forehead and his broad smile. She understood he had years of experience in large-scale operations with hefty budgets, but he didn't look anything like the stereotypical image of an accountant. "But like any construction project, you often don't know the impediments until they are in front of you. That slows things down and usually involves more money."

Amanda had no experience in that arena and just agreed ruefully with his observation.

"What seems to be lacking at this point is what the interior will look like."

"I thought there were plans to have a certain number of examination rooms in addition to the waiting room?" she asked.

"Yes, but I'm talking about the design of the reception space and the decoration of those rooms. I'd like your opinion on how they should look."

She didn't say anything for a moment then blurted, "It needs to be welcoming and cheerful. The families and their children shouldn't feel like they are charity cases and being treated less hospitably than the paying patients."

Barlow gave a big smile. "I was hoping you might say something like that. Which is why I would like you to head up the design of the interior."

She was stunned, pleased and, for once, speechless.

"I'd like to pay you as a consultant since the project is limited in scope and you know the state of our finances."

Amanda was about to comment that she knew nothing about interior design, but that wasn't strictly true. Her mother had signed her up for a class two years ago as a slight nudge to have her daughter thinking about how to decorate a home. That wasn't at all the same kind of project as a waiting room and clinical exam rooms, but hadn't she just declared that the space should look welcoming? Perhaps like a home in some way. And in a great leap of confidence, she agreed to take on the task.

"I think I'll do some research at the library and see if I can find photos of what other hospitals have done," she said.

He raised his eyebrows. "I don't know if that kind of information is readily at hand. The few journals about hospital administration are strictly about that topic and don't bother themselves with the aesthetics of the interiors. But I welcome you to give it a try. The Board meeting is at the beginning of the week if that's not too soon to share your initial thoughts and get some responses from them."

She thanked him and left his office, her mind reeling with ideas, and she couldn't wait to meet her father for lunch to tell him all about it.

Chapter 2

Edward Burnside was a member of several men's social clubs in Boston and often used their dining rooms for business purposes and connections. However, the clubs were strictly men-only, so he chose to dine with Amanda at their favorite seafood restaurant close to the harbor. He was already seated when she came in, her cheeks rosy from the cold and full of the energy that she had been lacking recently.

She kissed him on the cheek and sat down, brimming with her news.

"You'll never guess what," she began.

"I'm sure I can't."

"I've been offered a job."

Her father, who was practiced at masking emotion, had no expression when he asked her to elaborate.

She was so excited about the prospect of doing something new that she launched into a long description of how the opportunity came her way, how she planned to find out all there was to know about design and how this could be the start of some new direction in her life.

"How much do they intend to pay you?"

"Oh. I forgot to ask." She laughed. "I didn't want to sound crass and to be honest, I would do it for free, just to have the pleasure of contributing something to the clinic."

Edward smiled at his daughter, who was usually more hardheaded and practical so perhaps this was a good turn of events.

The waiter brought them coffee and took their order for the best clam chowder the city had to offer before continuing their conversation.

"How do you propose to begin?"

"I thought I would pop into to the Public Library and ask for some help in locating what I'm looking for. I know that sounds vague, but librarians are notorious for interpreting what you can't express when you're searching. There must be photos of modern medical facilities, wouldn't you think?"

"I have no idea and I haven't been inside that library for years. I'm up to my ears referring to law books as it is. Have you thought about contacting someone in the design business? An architect or a decorator? Or the Massachusetts College of Art and Design? I know the Dean there and he might have a suggestion or a referral for you."

Amanda thought a moment. "Those are good ideas, and I will follow up on them, but I want to formulate my thoughts first about the concept and the tone of the project."

Her father nodded. "That's always a wise beginning. What is your goal? How do you hope to achieve it? It's how we always approach projects at the firm."

"I wish I had a paper and pen with me to scribble down some of the ideas racing through my head. But I'll wait until later."

He smiled and turned the conversation to a topic that was more in his realm of knowledge, the resolution of a complicated estate distribution. While Amanda listened and uttered comments from time to time, she was entirely out of her depth and let her mind think about how far she could take her project without rocking the Board's boat.

THE BOSTON PUBLIC LIBRARY was not too far away and by the time she had driven there and parked her car, she had some idea of how to phrase what it was she was looking for. The large reading room with its table lights was dim and she wondered if there was enough illumination to peruse whatever books or magazines she could find. Her first stop was the information desk, where she tried to articulate what it was she was looking for to an attentive middle-aged woman.

"We have many design books with excellent drawings and photographs, but they are not on this floor. Here, look for this Dewey decimal number when you get up to the correct floor. Take a chair near the windows for the best light."

Amanda walked up the wide staircase, wondering how long it had been since she was in this building and if she still had an active library card. Well, hopefully she wouldn't have to lug an armful of books home; she just wanted to get a taste of what there was. And it was a lot. Shelves upon shelves of books on architecture, history of design, decoration and home furnishing. It was overwhelming. Rather than stand in the stacks leafing through books, she decided to take a few to the end of the row to the light-filled tables near the windows. Many people were seated at the small tables, more than she would have expected for mid-afternoon and, as she passed the back of one man, he called out to her softly.

"Is that Miss Burnside?"

She turned in astonishment to see Detective Halloran with an open book and a pad of paper beside him.

"What are you doing here? Is this where the police department does research on crime and criminals?"

"I'm brushing up on my Latin."

"Are you planning to go into the priesthood?" she asked.

"Not anytime soon," he answered, not knowing if she were teasing him or just curious.

"Plenty of those folks in our extended family."

Amanda didn't know how to respond.

"And what might you be doing here?" he asked.

"I'm trying to get some design and decorating ideas."

"Fixing up a new house?"

She felt herself coloring a bit and was annoyed at her reaction. "No. I have an assignment to help with the planning and décor of the Children's Indigent Clinic for Mercy Hospital."

"Well, well. Do you think they'll have enough of a budget for red velvet curtains and Turkish carpets?" He tried to hide a smile.

After that comment, Amanda thought he was a bigger snob in his own way than she was.

"While they renovate the exterior and build out the exam rooms, we plan on making the interior more welcoming. After all, the structure was originally a warehouse, and it feels like it. We'll make it more like home."

"I'm sure you'll give it your best," he said.

She didn't know if he was being kind or sarcastic so, instead of trying to come up with a cutting response, she just nodded and made her way to another table. Studying Latin? She should have asked him why. Was he planning on attending medical school? That was the usual reason people gave for learning Latin in the first place aside from people quoting classical phrases to one another to show off. Well, it was no business of hers and she became immersed in the images of how large, impersonal places were designed to a more human scale. For exteriors, this seemed to include trees or benches. Potted palms would be out of the question in a waiting room because they'd take up too much space, but there was no reason there couldn't be photos of trees or better, a mural on the wall.

Murals! That was it. She thought of the local bank branch that had a mural of the Pilgrims' landing and their first encounter with the Indians observing the scene from behind trees in the forest. Anytime she had been to that bank, which was seldom, she noticed people waiting in line and gazing at it. A good distraction. If she could find an artist who did such work, that would be an easy solution to decorating a large wall. Of course, the topic would not be Pilgrims. Perhaps animals and flowers.

She sat back and looked toward the row of desks and saw that Halloran had left, but her mind quickly switched to thinking about what else would be appropriate for a parent and child waiting area. Another sudden thought came to mind: why not ask them?

She left the books on the desk for the librarians to shelve and went back to the hospital, where the clinic had been temporarily relocated during renovation. The nurse at the reception desk was surprised to see her, but Amanda explained why she was there and was happy to see about half a dozen mothers, some with more than one child, trying to manage them while making conversation with a neighboring parent.

"Excuse me," Amanda began, and they all fell quiet. "My name is Amanda Burnside and I'm working on a project to enhance the waiting room of the clinic when they are finished with the exterior renovations. I was wondering if you could help me." She paused, having learned that asking for help often put people in a cooperative mood. "I'm not a mother myself," she began but was interrupted by a hefty woman who had not bothered to take off her thick overcoat even though the room was warm.

"I could tell that. You don't have any food stains on your clothes."

That got a good round of laughter as some of them drew back a lapel to demonstrate the effects of cooking, cleaning and feeding children. Amanda laughed at the joke directed to herself with genuine humor.

"It must be quite a full-time job." She noticed they were now taking in the quality of her red coat and the brown suede gloves, and she hoped they didn't think she was trying to be Lady Bountiful and become embarrassed by that comparison.

"What do you think would be helpful to you mothers when you bring your children in?"

"A leash," one answered to laughter.

"I tell you, my older boy was such a hellion that we did have a leash for him. More of a harness," she added.

"What about a ringmaster like in the circus to control the lot of them?"

"No, seriously," Amanda persisted.

"Having a playpen for the littlest ones would help. It's hard with one in your lap and the other one wanting to run around but being told to stay still."

Others nodded their heads.

"They might be able to play with another toddler that way," one woman said to mixed reaction. Amanda thought the original idea was good but wondered about the risk of spreading infection between families if more than one child at a time were contained in that way.

"What about if we provided some toys, or books or puzzles?" Amanda asked, knowing she could get them donated if not salvaged from the attics of her friends.

There was a moment of quiet from the women and some looked at each other as Amanda wondered if she had misstepped somehow.

"Our children have plenty to keep them busy at home," said one.

"Of course, but when they're here there's often a wait and they get impatient. We could just supply a few things to keep them out of your hair." Amanda hoped that she had mollified whatever unintentional slight had been made.

"Mrs. Reagan, the doctor will see you now," said a nurse who emerged from the hallway and one of the women got up.

"Thank you for your suggestions," Amanda said, standing up, sensing it was a good time to leave.

"Thank you," Mrs. Reagan said as she passed by on her way into the appointment.

IT WAS a distracted drive for Amanda as she realized how little contact she had had with the clients of the clinic. She had collected paperwork to be filed in deep storage when their limited cabinets got full, shuffled through invoices and receipts that were sent via interoffice mail to other departments in the hospital and had even planned the previous year's Valentine Ball in support of Mercy Hospital. But the majority of that work had been done on the administrative floor of the main building because the space she could use at the clinic was so ill-lit, drafty and noisy due to the lack of actual ceilings in the rooms.

She had observed the women—there were never men bringing children in—and took in their sturdy shoes, determined faces and barely disguised frustration at having to corral more than one child while having to soothe a sick or fussy baby. She couldn't imagine juggling all that and then going home and preparing a meal for the family, doing the washing, the cleaning and whatever else people in working-class households had to do themselves. The things that were magically done in her home by maids, the cook and other servants. From what she had observed driving through those working-class neighborhoods from time to time, clotheslines were strung across the streets with laundry drying. She couldn't imagine the embarrassment of having her underclothing billowing in the breeze for all to see. And children were most often playing in the middle of the street despite there being a steady stream of cars and trucks.

When she got home, she decided to pop in on her sister who, due to her studies, might be able to help her find the best approach to dealing with people with whom she had so little contact. Louisa's bedroom door was closed so Amanda tapped softly in the event a nap was taking place but instead was met with, "Come in."

She was propped up in bed, reading a fashion magazine, and smiled at her older sister.

"To what do I owe this honor?" she said, patting the bed for Amanda to sit down. Somehow, in the last few months, the tables had turned between the sisters where Louisa now seemed to be the more confident person while Amanda had been searching for a purpose in her life.

"Magazines? Shouldn't you be boning up on your studies?" Amanda asked, exerting her older sister persona.

"The classwork is a breeze. No problems there at all," she answered, putting the magazine down.

"I don't know how to phrase this exactly, but have you done any fieldwork so far? Such as visiting homes or talking to the folks you'll be dealing with?"

"What an odd question!" was Louisa's response.

"Aside from the random anecdote you share at dinner about a person you may have encountered on public transportation, I mean. I suspect you only do that to get Mother wound up, but that's another story altogether."

Louisa giggled. "That last part is true. You remember how horrified she was when she learned I was seeing Rob Worley, the owner of a club. The horror! Until she met him and found out he is a decent, hardworking man."

"By which you mean you are still seeing him?" Amanda asked.

"Discreetly, of course."

"Naturally. At the club?"

"Sometimes."

"Be very careful. If Mother and Daddy find out you two are still an item, you may be locked up in your room until Doomsday with only magazines to keep you company."

Louise looked away in disdain then turned her gaze back on her sister. "Is that what this chat is all about? Big sister romantic advice?"

"No, sorry. The conversation veered off in that direction. What I wanted to know was—well, I have been given a job."

"What? Do the parents know?"

"Daddy does. It's a short-term job, an assignment, really. And it involves trying to make the clinic a more appealing place for women and their children to wait for their appointment without pandemonium or mothers glaring at their young ones who have nothing to do. I thought it would be a good idea to talk to some of those mothers today, and I did, and I feel as if I may have stepped on some toes."

"You?" Louisa laughed.

"I know I am more direct than most women, but how could I find out what their needs were if I didn't ask them? What do you think those mothers want while they are waiting to be see the doctor?"

"Fashion magazines?" Louisa asked.

"You're hopeless," Amanda said, getting up. "I don't know how you expect to learn anything when I never see you cracking a book, much less going to classes." She glanced over at Louisa's desk and only saw stationery rather than textbooks and notebooks.

"Some people don't need to study as hard as others," Louisa said, resuming her perusal of the magazine by flipping over another page.

Amanda made a face of annoyance at her sister's attitude just as her mother appeared at the open doorway.

"What's going on?" she asked, looking up at her older daughter who was much taller than she.

"Just needling each other, that's all, Mother."

"What's this I hear about a job?"

"Daddy's home already?" Amanda asked, leading her mother back down the hall.

"Yes, and I'm very concerned about his news. I don't know if I like you being in that neighborhood where the hospital is located. It's one thing when you're in the main building but out and about in that dreary clinic…."

"That's what the job is. Making the dreary clinic more cheerful and pleasing."

They went down the stairs together to the sitting room, where a fire was lit and her father sat in one of the armchairs.

"Thanks for spilling the beans," Amanda said to her father, who smiled sheepishly in return.

"And the slang that you've picked up. Honestly!" Her mother sat in a chair opposite her husband while Amanda was adjacent on a loveseat next to a table with a small statuette of Diana the huntress.

"Now look at this brave woman," Amanda said. "I'll bet her parents weren't upset that she picked up a bow and went hunting for dinner." She ran her fingers along the length of the small bronze reproduction.

"Who were her parents, anyway? Oh, I've forgotten so much more than I ever learned, I believe," her mother said.

"Jupiter and somebody or other. The usual story," Amanda said.

The maid Nora came into the room with a look of concern on her face but stopped short in front of the three.

"What is it?" Margaret Burnside asked.

"There was a policeman who called when you were all unavailable. He said it seems that someone tried to break into the neighbor's house."

"Which one?"

"The Armstrongs. Someone saw a man sneaking about the back garden and called the police. He ran off before they arrived. The policeman wanted you to know to be careful to lock up the doors at night although, of course, we always do."

"Thank you, Nora," Mr. Burnside said, picking up the newspaper and shaking his head at the information.

"What's happened to this city? It used to be so calm and safe and now even Beacon Hill is swarming with strangers," Margaret said. She glanced over at her daughter with concern, clearly referring to their earlier conversation.

"I'll be very careful, Mother. It's a short-term task that I will be performing, and I won't be in any danger, I can assure you.

Chapter 3

Amanda made sure to get up and out of the house as early as possible the next day, leery of her mother's nagging concerns. Miss Bailey was the only person on the administrative floor when Amanda arrived with a sketchbook tucked under one arm.

"Are you going to the museum today?" the receptionist asked.

"No, just putting on paper some ideas I've had," Amanda answered.

She settled herself in the small office that was allocated to the volunteer women, opened the pad to a clean sheet and began to draw a simple three-dimensional rectangle that represented the clinic's waiting room. She realized she didn't have the exact dimensions, but this was only a mockup, not the actual final product. Chairs were positioned around the periphery of the room with a cage-like playpen in the middle for the babies. But where could the mural go if the chairs were up against every wall? She thought back to the scene of the women in the waiting area when she spoke to them and realized that the chairs were positioned back-to-back in short rows, a much better use of space than along the walls. Reproducing that scheme, she saw that it afforded the ability for the women and their children to talk and interact, which was surely what could best occupy their waiting time.

She became frustrated not knowing how much space she had to work with and decided to put her coat back on and go down to the construction site and see for herself if the new waiting room had the same dimensions as the pre-renovation one. Even if it were not yet built out, she could ask the foreman about the measurements.

Walking out the back doors of the hospital she was hit with a blast of cold air and huddled down into her coat further, wondering how the workers could stand the elements day after day in all seasons. Once again, there was the ash can with a fire burning in it and a few men drinking from a thermos while leaning against the shed. They nodded as she approached and she saw that they were probably not as large as they appeared; rather, they had several layers of clothes on under thick woolen coats, their heads protected by scarves and knitted hats.

"Hello, is the foreman here?" she asked the first man she walked up to.

He raised his eyebrows in question.

"The foreman? The boss?"

He jutted a thumb in the direction of the building, and she saw he had on gloves with the fingertips cut off, surely better for work but hardly enough protection from the cold. She was reminded of children coming into the clinic with chilblains and wondered how their parents allowed them to get to that state. Probably they didn't have enough heat in their apartments and likely were playing outside without gloves on.

She walked up to the open doorway of the building and could hear hammering at the far end of the hallway lit by a string of lights on an extension cord that ran from a generator chugging away outside.

"Hello?" she called out.

A big man dressed similarly to the workers outside came out of what used to be one of the exam rooms and walked quickly up to her.

"No clinic today. Main building," he pointed back to the hospital.

"I'm not here for the clinic. I work for Mr. Barlow and I'm here to look at this room."

"What? Why?"

"I need to see how big it is so we can buy the correct furniture," she said.

He looked puzzled but motioned her to follow him back to the place from which he had come. It was behind one of the standing walls of the reception area, but instead of the small exam room there was now a much larger space since they must have taken down some separating walls. There was an electric heater humming and giving off just enough heat to be bearable and a large table with drawings partially rolled up. He made a motion with his hands as if to ask if this was what she was looking for and she nodded.

Amanda couldn't make heads or tails of what she was looking at. The pages contained drawings in blue ink of horizontal and vertical lines with notations at the sides which made no sense to her. Why couldn't they just write, twelve feet by twelve feet or whatever size the room was meant to be?

"Do you know if the reception area is meant to be the size it is now?"

He sighed, said, "Wait here," and disappeared out to the hallway. A few minutes later, he returned with a similarly dressed man and pointed in my direction.

"Hello, I'm Amanda Burnside and Mr. Barlow has asked me to take a look at the construction site."

"What for?" he said in a combative tone, not giving out his name.

"He's asked me to do some decorating of the reception room, only I don't know if you intend to keep it the same size or if that wall will come down, too."

He looked as if he couldn't be bothered by her silly questions. "I don't know. I'm the boss of the men here. I don't do no drawings."

"Who could I talk to about this?" she persisted.

"Ask Mr. Barlow. I don't know."

He either didn't know or didn't want to bother talking to her anymore and he gestured to the open doorway, indicating the conversation was over. Amanda was frustrated by his attitude and the annoying fact that he either didn't speak English well or pretended not to understand. She began walking back to the main hospital and saw a familiar man in a suit and overcoat with an oversized portfolio case coming toward the clinic and she stopped him.

"Emerson, what are you doing here? Are you somehow involved with this project?"

He chuckled. "I guess so. I work for the architectural firm that designed it."

"What happened to the financial job you had last year?"

"Everyone said it was a terrible time to take that job and they were correct. I never should have left my position as the hospital's accountant. But seeing how things turned out...."

"You were certainly not to blame for any of the events or Doctor Pembroke's behavior," Amanda said. What puzzled her was that Emerson was engaged to one of Amanda's old friends, Valerie, who had said nothing about his change of employment, nor had she cemented her plans for a wedding. Perhaps she or her parents were wary of her fiancé's ability to provide a living for them both. Now Amanda's curiosity was piqued, and she planned to politely quiz their mutual friends about the situation.

"You know I am still volunteering with the hospital," Amanda said. "I'm helping the new Executive Director plan out the décor of the interior of the clinic."

"That's good of you. How is the new man?"

"Very easy to work with. He's not a doctor, rather an administrative professional and he grasped the reins immediately. I was just looking at the work in progress here and trying to get an idea of the projected dimensions of the lobby to make some suggestions."

"I can help you with that," he said cheerfully. "I was just about to deliver more drawings and I'm sure I can dig through the pile to find the right one." Whatever his future job prospects, Emerson was unfailingly upbeat and helpful to Valerie's friends.

They went back inside the cold interior of the clinic, and he looked around at the bare walls. "Gosh, it looks huge, doesn't it? I got the impression that they were going to keep the walls up that separate this area from the hallway. I don't know if they are load-bearing walls or how the decision was made, but the hospital seemed anxious to keep the costs as low as possible while still achieving their aims."

He must have visited the construction site before because he walked directly to the room where the plans were laid out, the only room with a modicum of heat. He put his portfolio down and leafed through the drawings on the table, finally rolling many over to his left as he located the one he was searching for.

"Here, this is it. There is no indication of a tear down, but luckily, I have my trusty slide-lock tape measure in my pocket." He pulled out the device and walked into the other room and began to measure along one wall, extending the metal to its full length and then scuffing a mark on the dirty floor and beginning again until he had walked all the way to the facing wall.

"Bigger than I would have imagined," he said, giving her the measurement in feet before measuring the width in the same manner. "That's some square footage."

"It won't look so big once the reception desk is put in and the chairs for the waiting patients. I can tell you that it is a busy place every time I have come here. Thank you, Emerson, that will help a lot."

"This is a solid ceiling here, but in some buildings, it's faced with tiles and if you know the size of one tile, all you have to do is count how many tiles there are. Presto!"

"How clever. Do you think you want to study architecture?"

He blew out his cheeks in exasperation. "I've already got a bachelor's degree and I don't envision going back to school for another discipline. But I can work my way up in the business and learn design without being licensed as long as I don't call myself an architect."

"That sounds like a good plan. This financial Depression won't last forever, and people will start building again," Amanda said, not really believing relief was coming anytime soon.

"It's a job and I like it. We'll see."

Armed with the new information about the dimensions of the room she was to design, Amanda went back to her office in the hospital, not before taking a good look at the layout of the various reception areas in the main building to get an idea of how they were set up. Her mind was whirling with ideas, and she couldn't wait to fill in the mostly blank sheet of paper that was waiting on her desktop.

Chapter 4

Amanda had a busy week of looking in the Yellow Pages for furniture stores and trotting around looking for something suitable for her project, only to find that what was needed was functional and industrial, not home furnishings. She got the name of several companies that produced just such items and wondered what had become of the old chairs. Were they stored somewhere in the hospital building, or had they taken off on their own legs to someone's home? She couldn't imagine who would want those uncomfortable things unless they had been spirited away for resale; she would investigate in the following days. She had made up her mind to alleviate that institutional feeling with a more cheerful paint color and hadn't yet given up on the mural, either.

When the weekend arrived, Fred, who put in so many hours at the hospital, found the one time they could go to a musical performance, which turned out to be Early Music on Saturday afternoon. It was a usual cold January day, but the sun was out, teasing them with the hopes of an early spring, and they decided to walk to the Orpheum Theater on the other side of Boston Common from their respective Beacon Hill homes. It was comfortable to stroll arm in arm, talking about his work and her project although avoiding any topic that had to do with future relationship plans. As he chatted to her, she realized that she had been comfortable all her life and was looking to do something more challenging. It was expected that she continue on the course she had been set on by a family of status, social connections, wealth: top-notch boarding school, coming-out party, volunteer work and the next step, marriage. And at her very side was a person that would fit the bill in rounding out her life's path, a professional man from a good, if somewhat eccentric, family who would provide her with something similar to the home and life in which she had grown up. That was all very nice but—and she didn't know what the alternative to that might be. Not yet.

Early Music turned out to be something new to her ears, used as she was to the classical repertoire when she attended the Symphony. Even the venue was a bit strange since the Orpheum was a movie theater but somehow had made an exception for this group of enthusiasts, many of whom knew each other. The program was composed of pieces she didn't recognize, and it took a bit to get used to the different sound from the non-modern instruments, the rhythms and the style of singing. But soon she could imagine herself a courtier in someone's palace listening to a performance enhanced by the costumes worn by the performers.

There was an intermission and Fred introduced her to some of his acquaintances before excusing himself, leaving her to discover that none of them were doctors, but either former university classmates or people he had met through their mutual appreciation of the music. There was a lawyer who recognized Amanda's surname since he was familiar with her father's legal specialty. That led to a long discussion about estate planning, and a woman who overhead them came up and had questions of her own. She was beginning to wonder when the break would be over when Fred came back into the room.

"Is everything all right?" she asked, thinking he might not be feeling well.

"Probably something I ate," he answered. "How are you enjoying the concert so far?"

"It's entirely new to me," she said. It was eye-opening to know how many interests Fred had which she knew nothing about. She was aware his family had some peculiar members—his mother in particular—but this shone a different light on his personality and the breadth of his intellectual life.

It was already beginning to be dark when they started to walk home along Park Street where there were streetlights, but the traffic, with horns honking and a truck backfiring, made it almost impossible to hear one another. Fred had the idea to cut through Boston Common to shorten the distance. There were lights there, too, although more sparsely located, but the dense vegetation had the advantage of reducing the biting wind that had picked up and it was certainly less noisy. They huddled closer for warmth.

"I'd be a hopeless Arctic explorer," Amanda said.

"I don't imagine any of those folks try to explore with only sheer stockings on their legs," he responded.

"When I was a little girl, I routinely wore leggings in the winter. But then when I got to a certain age other girls called you a baby if you appeared at school with them on. Hence, the first argument with my mother about what I should and shouldn't wear. I won and have suffered ever since. Are my legs cold? Yes, they certainly are and that's why I am walking so quickly." They heard a dog barking not too far away, not an unusual sound in that location.

"I'd be happy to go faster. And not in the least embarrassed if you chose to revert to wearing wool leggings. I wouldn't call you a baby." They increased their speed, and their path took them closer to the sound of the dog, a Boston Terrier, that came running toward them, barking and trailing a leash behind him.

"Oh, dear, he must have escaped and with it being so dark, he'd be hard to see," Amanda said.

As they approached, he stood his ground and barked, turned and ran back from where he had come.

Fred gave chase and Amanda tried to keep up in her heeled boots, hoping she wouldn't slip on a patch of ice. She could hear him calling after the dog, but the barking had ceased. She came around a turn and saw Fred standing hands on hips watching a retreating figure.

"Is that the owner?" she asked.

"I don't know. It looked like that hobo I've sometimes seen around here. That doesn't mean it's not his dog. The animal ran right up to him, and they both took off."

Amanda could just see the bulky figure walk quickly away and then veer off the path so as not to be seen under the lights. Fred shook his head, and they resumed walking, Amanda with her chin down towards the scarf around her neck, feeling the cold. Something caught her eye.

"What's that?" she asked pointing to an evergreen bush where something lay.

They stopped and Fred approached. "It's a person. Hello? Are you all right?" He touched the shoe and then the lower leg.

"If he's asleep out here, he'll freeze to death," Amanda said, following onto the grass.

Fred had already pushed the branches of the bush aside, knelt down and was busy talking in soft tones to whomever it was. He stood up.

"There's no need to worry about that. He's already dead."

They stood looking at one another.

"He's been shot."

"How is that possible? We should have heard it," Amanda said.

"There's no telling how long ago it happened. Not yet. First, we must get the police here. I don't want you walking out of the park by yourself to get help, but I also don't want to leave you here with this fellow in the event someone may think he didn't do a proper job of it and come back."

Their attention was caught by a person coming down a path from a different direction who slowed down as he saw a man and a woman standing in the grass.

"Hello!" Fred called out. "We need some help. I'm a doctor and I just found someone here near the bushes who appears to have died."

The person was a small man who said nothing at first and assessed the scene.

"You want me to get the police?" he asked.

"Yes, that would be very helpful. We don't want to leave him here, but neither do we want to send one of us out alone on that mission. Do you know where the nearest police station is?" Fred asked.

"No, but I know there are several cops on patrol around the Common when it gets dark. Let me see if I can rustle someone up." He took off toward the street where they had been headed.

"It's a major intersection," Fred said. "There is bound to be someone there, perhaps directing traffic."

"I guess we just wait," Amanda said, feeling the cold even more now that they weren't walking. Fred put his arm around her and offered to give her his scarf, but she declined. She couldn't allow him to be colder than she.

"I'll be fine," she said.

Their wait was only about ten minutes and the man who had encountered them came back with a patrol officer in tow. There were introductions and explanations and then the officer looked down at the body to see for himself.

"My partner on the street is already heading to the station and they'll bring back others in a little bit." He was dressed in a thick woolen coat with ear muffs, scarf and gloves yet still he stamped his feet in the cold.

"It must be rough being on the night shift," Fred said.

"Mercifully, I don't do it all the time," he answered with a touch of brogue. "Someone got sick, and I was next in line. It's only for tonight. What are you two doing walking through Boston Common in the dark?"

"It's my fault," Fred said, hanging his head a bit. "We were at a concert of Early Music, and I thought that this might be faster than following the main streets with the wind so fierce and the traffic noise."

The officer obviously had no idea what Fred was talking about and couldn't understand why he would have chosen to take his lady friend into the park area at night but made no comment.

"Help will be on the way in a bit," he said, just to say something.

The way the officer looked at Amanda suggested that he thought she ought to reconsider a choice of companion. Her first reaction was, what business was it of his? Her next reaction was, what *am* I doing out here on a freezing night in January standing only feet away from a dead body waiting for the police to arrive? Surely, they would want to interview her and Fred and all she could think of was that her legs were very cold, and she was getting hungry, and the night ahead would be long.

Not too much later, a car drove onto Boston Common on the very path—which was not a street or drive—where they stood. To Amanda's surprise, it was Detective Halloran who exited the car. There was that awkward moment where he hesitated, then regained his composure and nodded to each of them, having met Fred only once, in the aftermath of the Valentine Ball incident.

"Miss Burnside," he said.

"Good evening," she said, trying to maintain her dignity despite shivering.

"If you would like to wait in the car, I'll take a quick look at the person you found," he said.

He intended to escort both to the warm car with the engine running and heat still on, but Fred insisted on staying behind to accompany the detective, sharing with him his observations and pointing to the gunshot wound. The other officer opened the car door for Amanda, who sighed as she felt the warm gust of air in the spacious back seat.

"Good evening, ma'am," said the officer behind the steering wheel. "Heck of a night to be standing around in the cold."

"I'll say," she said. "I don't know how you folks do it when you're on a beat out in this weather."

"Ah, we're tough old buzzards," he said in a thick Boston accent. "You'd be surprised what you get used to. Anyways, it's usually the young guys they put on foot patrol unless you get in trouble for something." He laughed,

Amanda was just about to ask if he had ever been in trouble, but the approach of Fred and Detective Halloran interrupted that train of thought. The officer rolled down the window and Halloran said that an ambulance would be arriving soon and that they might as well wait in the warm car until that occurred. They got in and Fred took her hand in reassurance, and she shivered not just realizing how cold he had become but at the thought that they might have barely escaped being shot themselves.

"Did you tell him about the hobo?" Amanda asked him.

"What hobo?" Halloran asked turning from the passenger seat to look at her.

"We heard a dog barking, and it approached us, then ran away. The next thing we knew, a man—I think it was a man—had the dog by the leash and scurried away into the dark," Fred explained.

"You think he was the guy that shot this man?" the officer asked, looking at them in the rearview mirror.

Fred looked at Amanda. "I don't know. We didn't hear a shot, but we hadn't been on the Common very long. We detoured because it was so noisy out on the street. The traffic could have masked the sound of a shot. The body was cool, not cold, so the autopsy will tell how long it's been since he died with some degree of accuracy."

The officer looked taken aback by Fred's commentary before Halloran said, "He's a doctor."

It wasn't very long before the ambulance arrived, and Fred and Halloran got out of the patrol car to be present when the body was put on a stretcher, the detective scanning the area with a flashlight and only coming away with a hat. The ambulance left and Amanda could tell by Fred's posture that he would have liked to go with them but, after a brief conversation with Halloran, returned to the patrol car.

"Do you feel up to making a statement tonight or would you rather come in tomorrow?" the detective asked them.

Amanda and Fred looked at each other and he spoke for them both. "We'd better do it now while impressions are fresh, don't you think? We didn't really see very much as it was."

She nodded and the officer behind the wheel managed to turn the car around as there was nobody walking on the path and not likely to be in that weather and drove slowly out to the nearest street. The station wasn't far away and not too far from Beacon Hill.

"Have you changed job locations?" Amanda asked, remembering that when she had encountered him the previous February, he was closer to the city center.

"Transfers happen all the time," he answered.

She noticed that the officer gave him a sideward glance and she wondered if there was a story was behind that relocation. When they got to the station, Halloran asked if they needed to use the facilities and then if they would like a hot cup of coffee. Yes, to both suggestions and once back in the lobby, they were escorted to a room together for a brief interview. The coffee tasted awful, but it was hot and received with thanks.

"We usually interview people individually, but since you're a couple and didn't actually witness the murder, I think we're safe doing it like this," Halloran said.

Fred seemed pleased by this definition of their relationship, but Amanda was peeved by his assumption. She let it go, knowing that any type of clarification would sound weird and possibly hurtful. After all, a couple meant two people.

Fred related their recent experience, looking to Amanda at key points for confirmation which she gave with a nod. When he said there was a dog barking, she clarified that it was a Boston Terrier and said even in the dim light she could see the leash was red leather. Fred looked at her in surprise and she shrugged.

"Women notice these things," she said.

The interview lasted less than thirty minutes, just enough time for the bitter coffee to grow cold. They were told that the statement—and they could both sign the one—would be ready sometime Monday if they could stop back in to do so. That was all.

"This is unusual, but under the circumstances, Officer Higgins will drive you back home," Halloran said.

Amanda could see that Fred was about to object so she put her hand on his arm and said, "We're not calling a taxi on a busy Saturday night and I'm not telling my parents where I am. Thank you, Detective, we would appreciate the lift."

Halloran looked down at her left hand on Fred's sleeve and noted her long, slender fingers and the absence of an engagement ring.

Chapter 5

Amanda had kept up her illusion of reserve and calm until she was deposited at her front door, Fred being taken to his mother's home next. She noticed that her hand was somewhat shaky as she fitted the key into the lock, which she attributed to the cold, but once inside the vestibule, she sat on the settle for a few moments, collecting her thoughts and breathing deeply to calm herself. She knew she was about to be besieged by her parents' concern about her late return and she would have to tell them the reason.

Sufficiently calmed, she opened the door to the sitting room proper and came face to face with Nora, the maid, who looked at her in surprise.

"You didn't ring the bell, Miss," she said.

"No, I let myself in."

"I'll take your coat," she offered.

"I'd better keep it on a bit longer, thank you. I'm properly chilled from the weather." It occurred to her for the first time that Nora, who usually left shortly after clearing the dinner dishes from the table, still had a long night ahead of her. She would tidy up, put on a sturdy overcoat and have to walk by herself to the nearest trolley stop, a few blocks away in that same bitter cold weather that Amanda had just experienced. For her, it had been this one night out in the cold; for Nora, it was every night in the winter, in the rain in spring and the heat in summer.

"Your parents are quite worried," Nora added, then stopped short, perhaps thinking she had spoken out of turn.

"I'm not surprised," Amanda said, taking off her hat and gloves and walking into the sitting room with its fire illuminating her parents on either side in their customary armchairs. They both stood up abruptly at her entrance and at once began quizzing her about what took so long, where was Fred, did they have an argument, what was the matter.

"Let's all sit down," Amanda said. "I think I may be in need of some of Daddy's 'tonic,' by which she meant his stash of whiskey, usually brought out for medicinal purposes only.

Margaret's eyes went wide, but she waited until her husband reached into the drum-like end table, pulled out the bottle and three glasses and poured an inch of the amber liquid. Amanda raised her eyebrows as he held out a glass and he retrieved it and doubled the amount. Her parents took a sip and Amanda more of a gulp.

"The concert was interesting. Early Music. I had no idea what it was but if we lived in medieval or Renaissance times, perhaps it would have been familiar. People in

period dress, instruments of that time—probably repro-
ductions—and enthusiastic performers and audience
alike."

Margaret looked at her husband with concern.

"Is that what has put you into a tailspin?" her father asked
calmly.

"No. On the way back, Fred suggested we cut through the
Common since the traffic on the street was so heavy and
noisy and it was calm inside the park. Until we came across
a barking dog and then a man who had been shot."

Margaret was too shocked to gasp and looked at her
daughter, who pretended nonchalance while sipping the
whiskey. Finally, she managed to say, "In front of your very
eyes?"

"No, the man had been shot before we came across his
body lying alongside some bushes."

"Edward!" Margaret said looking pointedly at her
husband.

"What do you imagine I can do at this point? Your
daughter has always been headstrong and now add to that,
reckless in walking about in the dark where felons and
murderers lurk. And we also have Fred Browne to blame
for a foolish and dangerous decision."

They were quiet a few moments, sorting through their
reactions.

"I'm surprised you are taking this so calmly," her father
said.

"I'm not," Amanda replied. "It was awful. I saw the body, but not too closely. Just knowing that he had been alive not too long before has shaken me to the core."

Her father got up from his armchair and sat beside her on the loveseat, putting his arm around her. Only then did she feel she could let go of her restraint and bend her head onto his shoulder and weep.

"My poor dear girl," he said.

Margaret began to cry as well and that was the only sound in the otherwise tranquil house.

"I'm thinking that perhaps you should stop your volunteer work with the hospital," she finally said.

"Why? What has that got to do with anything?" Amanda asked.

"Raising money for the hospital is a worthy activity. But you don't need to go to that part of town and actually be in the building."

"Mother, nothing like that has ever happened at the hospital. And what happened tonight was on the Common, blocks away."

"Well, that's not exactly true," her father said. "The hospital isn't in the safest of neighborhoods."

"I'm perfectly safe there," she insisted.

"That's because you're not walking around at night. What was Fred thinking? Now I begin to question his judgment. Here I thought he was a capable, conservative person, not someone with rash ideas and strange impulses," Margaret said.

"It might not have been a wise thing to take a shortcut through the Common at night, but it was hardly pitch dark. There are lamps lighting the paths. I didn't feel in danger."

"Until danger almost came looking for you," her father said.

"Dinner has been held up long enough. Let's get some food into you, then a hot bath and bed," her mother said.

Louisa was waiting in the dining room and had been apprised that something dire had happened but was not given any details by Nora or Mary, who had picked up bits and pieces of the incident as they went about their work. The other three family members came somberly into the room and sat down to a bowl of hot consommé while Cook's eye through the peephole into the dining room perceived that they would soon be ready for the main course.

It was an odd meal with almost no conversation as the talk would certainly lead back to the incident that troubled them. Louisa knew better than to ask any questions and upset the others; besides, she anticipated grilling Amanda later. She couldn't imagine what was so horrible that everyone was reduced to silence. Dessert was served and Amanda was about to excuse herself to run a bath and try not to think about the earlier part of the evening. The phone rang and Mary came to tell her that Doctor Browne was on the phone. Amanda assumed he wanted to know that she was all right and apologize for his actions, but she shook her head and put her hands next to her head pantomiming sleep. Mary nodded and relayed the message.

There was something therapeutic about soaking in hot water, her head wrapped in a towel, watching the steam rise from the water. She had seen dead bodies before and been pursued by people trying to kill her as well, so she couldn't rationally think why that incident bothered her so much. And what did this mean about her relationship with Fred, which was amiable and comfortable for her, but not romantic. Where her mother had once championed him as a good marital prospect, that had changed and now all she would see were faults. She would paint him as impulsive, irresponsible, related to a tribe of strange people, his mother the strangest of all.

There was a knock on the door that she knew to be Louisa since they shared the bathroom and no one else would think to interrupt a bath. She entered and sat on the small stool in front of a vanity table.

"Bad things, huh?" Louisa said.

Amanda nodded.

"We're blood sisters, right? I mean, obviously sisters, but you made me take that silly blood oath when we were children, pricking our fingers and mingling the blood."

Amanda gave a wry smile.

"To stand up for each other and cover for each other as need be."

Now Amanda's curiosity was raised.

"I'm sorry to admit at this late stage that I, too, witnessed the aftermath of a murder."

Amanda just stared.

"I was at Rob's club, and it was very noisy—"

"When was this?"

"Just a few months ago. And there was this popping sound which I thought nothing of except the entire place went quiet. Everybody in the room knew what that sound meant except me. Aldo ran out to the alley and for some reason, I followed him although Rob tried to hold me back. There, sitting down, propped against a garbage can was a man who had been shot in the forehead."

Amanda's eyes grew wide. "You never said anything!"

"How could I tell Mother and Daddy? Should I have said, 'I had a good day today and by the way, saw someone who got shot in the head.'?"

"What did Rob do?"

"He had to call the police although someone in the area had already done so. But first he had to rummage through some papers and put things in the safe."

"Like what?"

Louisa hesitated. "Money. In case the cops came in and decided to take it for evidence although it had nothing to do with what went on in the alley. And a gun."

"Who is Rob Worley? A clean, above-board club owner? Or is he involved in some other business that involves a lot of money and the need for a gun? And since when have you started to refer to the police as 'cops'?"

Louisa shrugged. "Not at home, of course."

"Okay, blood sister. Fess up. Have you really been going to social work classes at college?"

Louisa tried to look penitent. "No."

"What do you do all day?"

"I take the books with me, get notes from someone in my classes then go to the club."

Amanda covered her eyes with both hands. "I can't believe you are doing this."

"Well, blood sister, you have been sworn to lifelong secrecy and will not rat me out to Mother and Daddy."

"Rat you out? Please don't start talking like a gangster's gun moll in some movie. But I won't disclose what you've been up to as long as you take proper measures to protect yourself."

"Like getting my own gun?"

"No! Like not spending all your time at that club. Who was killed and why? Do you know?"

"Rob said it was nothing to do with him, per se. The man who was shot was part of some gang that was trying to shake him down."

"What does that mean?"

"Trying to make him pay for protection. A rival gang, which was trying to do the same thing decided that the guy needed to be stopped. It was also a warning that Rob needed to take the offer seriously."

"Protection from what? What does he do?" Despite the hot water, Amanda was feeling a chill down her spine.

"Protection from the gang and the police. They come around and ask for money or they will report Rob for what he is doing or hasn't even done."

In response to Amanda's gaze, Louisa continued. "In case you haven't figured it out, he runs a few speakeasies although the club is the legitimate business. Just music and food. No alcohol. That happens at different locations."

Amanda couldn't believe that her sister, the shy debutante at the previous year's Valentine Ball, was involved with— how could she describe him—a bootlegger, gangster, mobster? Her parents had been aghast when they first learned he owned a club but his dapper appearance, impeccable manners and educated demeanor had finally appeased them when he turned up at their beach house in Maine the previous summer. At that time, the worst insult they could hurl was calling him a band leader and owner of a club. Could they possibly imagine the actual breadth of his activities and that their precious younger daughter was not just involved with him but was fully cognizant of his activities?

Amanda managed to eke out a smile for her sister indicating that she would not be the one to tell their parents anything of their conversation. Louisa smiled back and left Amanda wanting to plunge her head, towel and all, under the water and forget about the entire day.

Chapter 6

The usual Sunday routine was set aside due to Amanda's incident, and Mr. and Mrs. Burnside attended church without their daughters. For the girls, it meant a sleep-in morning, although Amanda did not know why Louisa was able to enjoy the privilege, too. The thick **Boston Globe** was all theirs to read leisurely in their dressing gowns while lingering over cups of coffee.

"Have you ever thought of getting an apartment of your own?" Louisa asked out of the blue.

"I think it would be odd for me to live by myself when things are just fine here," Amanda answered.

"I meant, perhaps we could share an apartment."

Amanda put down the section of the paper she had been reading and gave her sister a hard look. "I could see how it would suit you just fine, but it would not be an advantage to me."

"Oh, come on. You could come and go as you like, not have to be punctual to dinner every night…."

"Not have the parents scrutinize whomever I was seeing, either?" Amanda said.

"You'll be coming into your money soon so you could well afford it," Louisa said, referring to trust income set up by their grandfather.

"Let's just wait until it's your turn to get your money and maybe then I'll consider it." Amanda rustled the paper back into shape and continued reading.

"That's fine with me although you'll practically be an old maid by then."

"I think you've been hanging around with jazz club society too much. Are you thinking you're missing out on all the fun because you have a curfew? I can't imagine how wild you would be without one." Amanda realized she was sounding a bit old-fashioned, but she felt she had to play the older sister role every now and then. She used to think that her responsibility was to encourage the previously quiet and shy Louisa to be more confident, but it seems her efforts had been taken too far.

"Well, I think it's an idea worth thinking about," Louisa said, picking up the society section of the newspaper. "My new friends are much more interesting that the X-Ds and their dreary talk about engagements, weddings and who knows what." She was referring to Amanda's friends from her debutante days and she wasn't far off from the truth. The ex-debutantes, X-Ds as they called themselves, met for a lunch once a month and those were exactly the topics of conversation.

"We also discuss fashion and world events," Amanda said, unable to subdue a laugh at her own ridiculous comment.

"I can imagine," Louisa said. "Unless they have been to Europe on their own tours, I am sure they have no clue where half of the countries that are in the newsreels are located."

"You're probably right."

"What are you going to do all day?"

"Mope around in my dressing gown, milking sympathy until Sunday dinner. Then I'll finish up the drawings for the clinic improvements. There's a Board meeting tomorrow and I get to make a presentation."

"How very exciting," Louisa said sarcastically.

HER SISTER MAY HAVE THOUGHT that her project was of no importance, but Amanda had taken the endeavor seriously. She had made several more trips to the interim clinic location and spoken to more women about what would make their appointments and waiting times easier and, after the expected round of jokes about child containment, they had a lot to offer. Ever since she began the project, she had taken to coming in their entrance to nod to some familiar faces and to observe how the space was used. The Monday morning of her presentation was no exception, and she came through the door juggling a portfolio with the drawings and pictures of furniture that various companies had supplied. To her great surprise, Nora was in the waiting room with a small boy.

"Oh!" was all Amanda could manage, wondering how she didn't know that Nora was married or that she had a young child.

"Good morning, Miss. Your mother kindly gave me the morning off so I could take my nephew Declan here."

Amanda said hello to the youngster who looked to be about four years old and very sad.

"He's had a terrible sore throat for a few days and is feeling miserable."

"I'm sorry to hear that," Amanda said, looking at him.

He nodded, acknowledging her concern as well as his pitiful condition.

"It could be tonsillitis," Nora whispered although Declan could obviously hear what she said. "My mother usually looks after him while my sister works, but she's feeling poorly, too."

"I hope it's not influenza," Amanda said. "It seems to come back every winter." Then addressing the little boy, she added, "I'm sure the doctor will find out what is wrong and fix it."

"Will he give me a lollipop then?"

Amanda had no idea if that was standard procedure and said, "I think you'll need to ask him."

She made her way up to the administrative floor thinking about all the juggling of schedules and time off work that some people had to contend with in order to deal with family illness. Amanda had no idea where Nora lived— once she left in the evening, it was as if she no longer existed until she appeared the next morning. How long a trip was it each way? What about this trip to the clinic with a sick child? And who was looking after Nora's mother? What if the little boy needed his tonsils out? Could the family afford the surgical fees?

The elevator doors opened, and she forced herself to think about the presentation she was about to give. She had long ago realized that anything that began with, 'I think' or 'I feel' would not carry any weight with this Board, having seen them previously disregard a female Board member who prefaced her comments in that way. Instead, Amanda had the idea of saying, 'According to scientific studies...' or 'Experts in the field have told me...' or 'It is common knowledge that..." And by no means was she going to state that any recommendations or decisions were based on her interactions with the poor families who had given their opinions. That was the road to disaster. Not just because her informants were poor, but also exclusively female and their points of view were of no consequence to the decision makers, no matter how liberal minded they perceived themselves to be.

Amanda was taking off her outer garments and unzipping the portfolio when Mr. Barlow put his head around the doorway and smiled at her.

"It looks like you are prepared for this morning. The meeting is not until ten—would you like to do a dry run, as they say?"

That hadn't occurred to her, but since he mentioned it, she thought it was an excellent idea. He could prepare her for what questions might come up, steer her away from issues that were not in her purview and suggest what points to emphasize. This would be novel since her only experience with presentations were formal recitations or readings in high school with each one done as an individual. Here he was proposing that this be a team effort and she felt buoyed by the suggestion.

Mr. Barlow took her back to his office and had her set up her materials on an easel just as she would during the meeting.

"Get there early and have it ready for viewing. The last thing anyone wants is you shuffling through papers looking for what you want to show them."

"Of course." She had the drawings and the pictures in the order in which she was going to discuss them and began speaking as if to the board. "Good morning. Mr. Barlow has asked me to research some improvements to the interior designs of the clinic. The first illustration—"

"Whatever you do, don't talk to the easel. You need to talk to your audience."

"Yes, of course."

"Make eye contact with them. Each time you make a statement, look at a specific person as if you are talking to him. Or her."

That too, hadn't occurred to her. She was hoping not to have to engage with some of the formidable figures who sat on the board.

"Better yet, why don't you have Miss Bailey help you tack up the images on the walls of the board room? The directors can look at them as they come into the room and be intrigued about what this all means. They will have had a look at everything before you begin to speak about it. Think: if you go whizzing through the pictures as you are talking, they may want to take a longer look at something while you are onto the next topic. If you have the images spaced around the room, you can speak directly to your audience while gesturing—do not point with your finger or use a pointer—to make your argument."

Amanda was dumbfounded. Why hadn't she thought of that? She wasn't reading a paper aloud about the role of Ophelia in Hamlet for an English literature class. She was presenting information to a group of decision makers and trying to guide them through words, supported by illustrations, of what path they should take.

She scurried to get Miss Bailey's assistance as well as cellophane tape and scissors and they began to put up the materials on the walls of the Board room in the order in which she would be speaking about them. They stepped back to admire their work.

"Pretty nice, if I say so myself."

Miss Bailey nodded solemnly, not her usual effusive demeanor.

"Why, what's the matter?" Amanda asked.

"I read in the paper about that man who was found on the Common," she said, and Amanda's heart clutched at the memory. "I sometimes take a short cut through there but it's the last time I will."

"Good." Amanda paused for a few moments before she revealed what she knew Miss Bailey would find out soon enough. "I have to tell you, the newspaper only said that he was found by two citizens. I'm afraid I was one of them."

Miss Bailey gasped and grabbed her arm. "How awful for you! To think such things go on in our city."

Amanda pulled herself together and said, "We'd better get back to work before the Board gets here. I'm sure you've got your own preparations to make."

"The minutes have been typed with copies made and the agendas are ready. I just have to spread them out on the table and get the pitchers of water and glasses." Here was a girl who was always ahead of schedule and Amanda could tell that Mr. Barlow was impressed by her work ethic.

Amanda was not nervous about her presentation but did have a touch of excitement that she hoped would be contagious. She had spoken before the Board the previous year about the progress of the Valentine Ball, whose organization was under the purview of the previous year's debutantes. What had always been largely a ceremonial post with some decisions made about the choice of flowers or menu and encouraging family and friends to attend—suitable training for a future society matron—had become a full-fledged exercise in project management including budgets and expenditures. Despite its being tossed in her lap due to other administrative circumstances in the hospital, she found she liked thinking on her feet and being decisive. Mr. Barlow hadn't even met her back then, but he clearly saw what she was capable of.

Shortly before ten, the Board members, some of whom she knew but others who had been newly appointed, began to slowly assemble. The Chair was now Mrs. Terrell, a hardworking member whose efforts had not been adequately appreciated in the past. The former Board Chair had also been the lead administrator, but there had been a change in the bylaws; those two positions had been split, effectively spreading the responsibility and creating a system of checks and balances. To date, it seemed to be working well and the addition of several new members had rejuvenated the group.

They greeted one another while removing overcoats and then, just as she had hoped, they walked around the room looking at the posted illustrations. Since they were all titled "Children's Clinic Improvements," they could surmise what some of the discussion would be about.

Mr. Barlow came in, followed by Miss Bailey, and after a few minutes, the meeting began. Amanda sat in the row of chairs behind the Board table and listened to the usual progress of events: roll call, approval of the agenda, approval of the minutes and then the treasurer's report, which had been prepared by Mr. Barlow, and discussion of possible donations from foundations that took an interest in medicine or health issues. There seemed to be new members who had direct links to those organizations and at that point Amanda saw the clever designs of Mr. Barlow when he had advised Mrs. Terrell earlier about certain business and corporate people who might be interested in serving on the Board.

After several more items on the agenda, Mrs. Terrell introduced Amanda, with whom she had had previous pleasant interactions, as someone who had done many good works for the hospital and was prepared to do another.

It was a wonderful boost to have that opening accolade, and Amanda relaxed and followed the advice that Mr. Barlow had given her. A brief thanks for their time, an even shorter comment on her connection to the hospital and then she explained that she had been tasked with investigating how to make the clinic a more pleasant environment for the families who used its facilities. She made eye contact with specific individuals as she spoke and held out her hand in a gesture to look at the illustrations that were posted around the room. In no time at all, she felt perfectly at home addressing a group of important and influential people as if she was one of them.

Amanda could feel herself blushing with pride from the compliments from the Board members when she had finished.

Mrs. Terrell said, "The Chair will entertain a motion for Mr. Barlow to continue the renovations of the clinic with the addition of the interior designs provided by Miss Burnside."

A motion was made, seconded and there was no discussion, but Mrs. Terrell added that she depended upon Mr. Barlow to allocate appropriate funds for the implementation. All said 'aye' and the Board went on to the next item.

Amanda discreetly left the room, intending to collect her illustrations later, but in the meantime allowing herself to feel the elation of having persuaded a prominent group of people to undertake a project she had designed. It was a heady experience for her, especially in an area for which she had no professional expertise. She went back to the small office and tried her best to concentrate on the paperwork before her, but her mind kept wandering off to what this small success meant. She hoped this wasn't the end of using her creative abilities and research skills. And if it wasn't, what was next? She allowed herself to daydream and before long, she could hear Miss Bailey and Mr. Barlow returning from the Board meeting.

She went out to thank Miss Bailey for her assistance earlier, but she was nowhere to be found. When she went to the ladies' room, she saw Miss Bailey sitting in the lone chair in the corner, crying into her handkerchief.

"What's the matter?" Amanda asked. "Did something happen at the meeting?" She wondered if a mistake had been made and she had been reprimanded in some way. It was something the former Chair would have done, in front of everyone, no less.

"I just got a phone call. The man that was found—that you found—on the Common is someone I know. He was the Director of the Buildings Department and married to an old friend from my hometown. I just saw him at an event two weeks ago. I can't imagine that someone would shoot him! He was walking his dog on Boston Common." She looked incredulous. "They don't live anywhere near there. What was he doing on a Saturday night walking his dog there?"

"I saw the dog. It was a Boston Terrier."

"Yes, that's the breed. I've been to their house in Brookline. That's a long way to take your dog for a walk."

"Doctor Browne and I saw someone take the dog away. At least, let's hope he is safe. Oh, Miss Bailey, I am so sorry for your friend's loss." She went to her and gave her a consoling hug. Could the killer have been the person that she thought was just a hobo? Her mind went back to the sight of the man and dog making their way along the path out from the beam of the light and disappearing into the darkness.

Chapter 7

Amanda knew that Detective Halloran had as much information as she could supply and now had identified the person who was killed, which didn't mean that she wasn't intensely interested in what explanations he might provide. She took the card that he had given her with his contact information out of her pocket and turned it over in her hands. Perhaps it was none of her business, but curiosity got the better of her and she impulsively picked up the telephone in her small office and asked the operator to put her through to that number. She felt nervous and debated whether to hang up before he might pick up—but didn't they have some method of tracing calls? Or was that just in the movies she had seen? Before she could make up her mind, he answered.

"Halloran here." His voice was crisp and official.

Amanda gasped a bit in surprise then said, "Hello, this is Amanda Burnside."

"Well, hello, Miss Burnside. I was wondering when you would call."

What did that mean? "I just heard that you identified the person that Doctor Browne and I discovered on Boston Common."

"Yes, that's true. You must have your ear to the ground to have learned that already." She could almost detect a smirk in his voice, but it was likely her imagination.

She lowered her voice although nobody could hear her in the small office down the hall from the main administrative activity. "Mr. Barlow's secretary told me about it. She said the man was married to a friend of hers. And that they lived nowhere near Boston Common."

"Brookline."

"Yes, that's what she said."

There was a moment's silence and Amanda blushed to think of her brash initiative to call him and essentially tell him what he already knew.

"Have you had any information on the man who took the dog?" she asked, thinking it could be a way out of the awkward conversation.

"As you can imagine, that's the least of our worries."

"Unless he was the person who shot—"

"Mr. Harris?"

"Yes, that was my thought." She was feeling more ridiculous by the minute.

"That's a sensible line of inquiry to follow. Thank you for that suggestion."

"Very well, goodbye."

She hung up feeling like a complete fool and wondered if he would turn to someone in his office and have a good laugh about the busybody young woman trying to play detective.

Suddenly, the room felt unusually warm. "I need some fresh air," she said aloud, knowing no one could hear her and relishing being out in the cold weather. Putting on her coat, she went out the front door of the hospital to the busy street, alive with pedestrians as the lunch hour neared and realized she could probably check in on the construction site as they might be taking a meal break. Walking around the side of the building took some time since the frontage was narrower and she was hit with a blast of cold air; she turned up the collar of her coat, much good that it did.

The site looked much as it did every day, a small fire lit in the lee of the structure but nobody in sight. As she approached, she could hear raised voices and by the sound of it guessed an argument was going on. She slowed down, still not being able to see anyone since they must have been on the other side of the building. She could make no sense of what was being said as no English was used, but if she could guess by tone alone, someone was being chewed out and resisting it loudly with a word that didn't need translation.

"No! Non l'ho fatto!"

By this time, she had come around the corner and seen the scene where the foreman's face was inches from the face of one of the workers with a back-and-forth dialogue going at lightning speed, the boss poking his finger into the chest of the other as he spoke. The others were standing well away as if to keep out of the line of his ire, but some movement alerted the verbal combatants that they were no longer alone. They froze mid-sentence and separated, the worker with signs of relief and the foreman with annoyance that quickly changed to an ingratiating expression.

"Miss Burnside," he said, all smiles. "How nice that you come to see the progress."

"Was I interrupting something?" she said, trying to look innocent.

"A little dispute between two of the workers about some tools. It happens all the time. People who work with their hands are very careful about their tools."

"Possessive?"

"Yes, that's the word." He was walking toward the entrance to the clinic, which forced her to follow him to continue talking, but she did take note of the other workmen cautiously watching them before turning back to whatever task was at hand. "Come in where it's warm."

Amanda noticed that both the exterior and the interior looked the same as it had the last time she had visited and wondered what it was these men did all day. As she looked around, she could sense his eyes on her, and he likely assumed she was assessing his work.

"I'm just the foreman," he said, holding his hands out as if there was nothing to be done about it. "The boss, Mr. Romano, he's the one to tell us what to do and when to do it."

"I'm not here to check on your work. I just wanted another look at the reception area to make sure that my ideas were still sound."

"What do you mean?"

"I've made some drawings—," she began, but he cut her off abruptly.

"No! You do not do the drawings. The architect does the drawings, and the boss tells us what to do next."

"Yes, I know that. I didn't mean architectural drawings, I meant design drawings for where the furniture will be placed and if there is still space for a mural."

His temper receded as quickly as it had risen, and he was all smiles again. "Sure, sure, it's the women who do the decoration. I bet it's gonna look good."

"It will. It will be the best-looking children's clinic in the city as soon as the rest of the work is finished."

His face had begun to fall into a scowl again and she was afraid he was going to either raise his voice or try to engage her in a shouting match.

"Thank you," she said, ending the conversation and hurrying outside to get away from him.

"Good day, Miss."

She walked quickly back into the hospital and saw Fred coming toward her, still in his hospital whites, his angular face in a broad smile. "There you are. I've been looking all over for you."

"Just went out to get some cold air in my face while listening to a lot of hot air from the foreman."

"Don't pay any attention to those men. In fact, I would rather you didn't interact with them at all."

Amanda was taken aback by his tone and waited for him to explain himself.

"That didn't come out the way I meant it to. I've dealt with people from countries of all origins, and some come from cultures of extremely polite behavior. Others express themselves more forcefully, if you get my drift. I happen to have encountered the foreman before when his son was admitted for a mastoid condition and the man had the worst temper I've ever seen. He screamed at me, and his wife yelled back at him and then the two of them got into a war of words, none of which I could understand, of course. It drew several nurses and doctors to the room to see what the matter was and all the time their son lay in the bed calmly, which suggested that this was a common occurrence. Then, like a light switch being turned off, the conversation stopped, and normal exchanges began again. I've never seen such a volatile person. At least, not one who was not deranged."

"Do you think he is?"

Fred laughed. "In his case, it might be a fine line." He took her arm and pulled her toward the wall out of the way of a gurney being wheeled by. "Why I was looking for you was to see if you were free for lunch. It seems my schedule has been busy today, I haven't had a moment to talk to you."

Amanda was happy to receive the invitation. "Now?"

"Let me just change so someone doesn't think I'm the milkman. I'll be back in just a few minutes."

Amanda sat in the waiting room watching the activity all around her and wondered what life as the wife of a doctor would be like. She would like to think that there would be steady hours, certainly a professional status and money wouldn't be an issue. But she knew the hours were anything but regular if he wished to continue working at the hospital. Should he go out on his own into private practice? His family was well known in Boston—sometimes not in the best light—but his personal reputation was spotless, and he was sure to attract patients who wanted to see someone of his social standing. What of their social life? Doctors were always called out on emergencies, they got pulled away from dinner parties, recitals and performances leaving the wife to find her way home on her own. And what would her role be? That was the one hurdle she had when she thought about marriage. It seemed like a portal through which she would step, never to return to her regular life. Perhaps that was the point.

"Ready?" Fred said, standing in front of her. "You look as if you were trying to solve a calculus problem in your head just now." He adjusted his tie and put on his hat.

"Yes, something like that."

"Where would you like to eat?

Before she had given it a moment's thought he suggested an out-of-the-way place she had never been to before. Somehow Fred always knew of interesting places where the owner recognized him and lavished him with the delicacies of the particular cuisine.

They walked arm in arm for a few streets before he asked her if she were cold and should he hail a cab.

"No, I'm fine," she replied. "Let's not take any shortcuts, though." She winced at having made that remark, but he seemed to let it roll off his back. "Just a few more blocks," he said.

They turned into a narrow alley that led them to an enclosed courtyard which could make for a pleasant place to sit in warmer weather as there was a tree planted in the middle, but the metal chairs were upended on round café tables.

Amanda gave him a sidelong look, wondering if he expected them to eat out there, but he pointed up to the second floor of a narrow building with a rustic sign that read, *Ma Maison*.

"Oh, French," she said happily.

"Country French—home cooking."

The dense smells of what might have been onion soup filled the stairwell as they ascended and once opening the inner door, they were overcome by the deep aromas and the warmth that emanated from the broad old-fashioned hearth. Hearing the door opened, a wide- hipped woman in old-fashioned clothing turned her red face and smiled.

"Doctor Browne! How nice to see you!" She spoke with the slightest of accents as she turned to stir whatever was cooking in the large iron pots suspended from a crane stretched across the fire and which could be swung in or out depending upon the degree of heat required. Amanda looked around to make sure she had not suddenly been transported back to another century but was assured by the dress of another couple sitting in a corner that she was indeed still in the year 1932.

"Where do you find these places?" Amanda whispered.

"Some of the owners are people I meet through patients at the hospital, and you know, you get talking to them and learn a lot about their lives." Amanda didn't know many doctors who did that except General Practitioners like John Taylor, Amanda's cousin's husband.

The owner, Madame Fournier, ushered them to a table overlooking the courtyard and the leafless tree, giving Amanda a twinkling smile and already putting two and two together. "And how is the young lady?"

"Très bien, merci," Amanda answered.

The smile Madame gave Fred indicated that she was in full approval of his choice of lunch partner and perhaps more.

"Today we have duck cassoulet, onion soup, and still some coq au vin. But first let me bring you some medicine." She took one last look at the bubbling pots and disappeared into the back room.

"The other interesting thing is that because I am rather lean looking, all these motherly types think I need feeding up. It's not such a bad deal."

"I know you've been living at your mother's place in Beacon Hill, but surely she sees that you have enough to eat with your erratic schedule," Amanda said. She had met his mother a few times and thought her one of the oddest people who managed to have two normal adult children. And one who was not, but that was another story.

"Of course, we have staff to take care of the normal household needs, but Mother doesn't exactly supervise them. Her mind and efforts are still firmly in the land of fiction."

Amanda raised her eyebrows thinking that he meant she was no longer lucid, and her reaction made him laugh.

"No, no. She is entrenched with her hero Alistair and his adventures on the moors eluding the evil English while trying to save his girlfriend—or maybe it's his wife now—from similar perils and the unwanted attentions of some wealthy old landowner who stole his patrimony."

"And here I thought you'd never read any of her books."

"I haven't. She is always throwing out ideas for plots and asking for input. It makes for disjointed dinner conversations at times."

Madame Fournier came back to the table with two ceramic beakers, an odd choice of dinnerware, until Amanda realized that they concealed a substantial amount of red wine.

"Now, what will it be?" she asked, placing a basket with half a baguette on the table along with a ramekin of deep yellow butter. Her apple red cheeks offset by a neat white headdress made her look like a Breton housewife, and Amanda glanced down to see if she wore wooden shoes. Alas, no.

"I'd love the coq au vin," Amanda said, and Fred chose the cassoulet.

"Don't want to be too aromatic for my patients," he said.

"Pah. How else will they know you are fortified for your work?" She cuffed him lightly on the shoulder and returned to oversee the pots then returned to the back kitchen.

"Santé" and they clinked their drinking vessels.

They were quiet a moment and Amanda sensed he had something to tell her as he fiddled with the silverware. "I heard your presentation to the Board went well."

"Yes. Mrs. Terrell was supportive as was Mr. Barlow. What a different atmosphere he has brought to the hospital." He nodded but continued to straighten out the knife and spoon.

"We've known each other some time," he said, looking up and smiling.

Amanda smiled back and sensed that The Question was about to be popped, as her friends put it. What she couldn't remember was how to stall to formulate an answer.

"We seem to have a lot of interests in common." He drew his elegant fingers across his brow and took a deep breath. "Amanda, would you consider being engaged? To me?"

Before she had a chance to answer, Madame Fournier had arrived with two steaming plates and exclaimed, "A proposal! In my little restaurant! Bonne chance!" The couple at the other table smiled at them. The owner plopped the plates down and kissed Amanda on both cheeks and was practically in tears of happiness when she did the same to Fred.

"She hasn't given me an answer yet," Fred said solemnly.

Their hostess could see she had made a tremendous blunder and bustled away into the back kitchen while the room fell silent with awkwardness.

"Would you like some bread?" he asked, breaking off a hunk for her.

"Thank you," she replied.

"For the proposal or for the bread?"

That brought an uncomfortable sigh from Amanda. "I wasn't expecting it."

"At all? Or just not at this moment?" When she didn't answer immediately, he suggested that she taste her food before it got cold.

"The food is wonderful. And I'm flattered you think of me in that way."

He gave her a soulful look and she felt terrible. "Is that the standard 'no' response?"

"I wouldn't know. No one has asked before. By the way, your food will be getting cold, and we don't want to have Madame exiled to the kitchen in embarrassment for the rest of the day."

That got a chuckle out of him. "I can't believe no one has asked you to be engaged before. A beautiful, accomplished woman such as yourself." He finally tackled his lunch, dunking a hunk of bread in the sauce.

"I seem to have attracted more impulsive men in my past who went directly to the marriage proposal with an elopement thrown in for additional romantic drama." She resumed eating.

"Anybody I know?"

"Now, Fred, a lady never reveals that sort of information."

And it was true that she had no intention of telling him of her past relationships. One was a dear old friend who thought their friendship would be the basis of a solid marriage; he was probably right, but she wanted to be madly in love with the man she would marry. The other was her friend Harriet's boyfriend who had gone off to college and who had never reconnected. Once he was about to graduate, he must have felt adrift and called her out of the blue and at the end of a fun-filled conversation, he blurted, 'Let's get married.' She considered that a cry of loneliness or a desperate attempt to reclaim old times. In either case, she didn't hesitate to politely decline.

"My God, I have made this so awkward for you. I am sorry," he said, taking her hand.

"Let's leave it like this for a bit, and we'll see where it goes," she suggested.

That made him smile and she could see the affection in his face and was desperate to change the subject.

She looked out the window at the courtyard. "Isn't that charming? I'll bet in the summer there are pots of geraniums and maybe even a cat prowling around."

"It is. Madame has the tables and chairs set up and it is just like being in Paris. Have you ever been?"

"No, somehow that opportunity escaped me. If the food is like this, my regret has just increased tenfold." Her meal was unlike anything she had previously experienced. Earthy, substantial, with so many layers of flavors that it was impossible to identify how it was made.

"The food in Paris is just as complex only more refined. It would be an excellent place for a honeymoon."

"Fred..."

They ate in companionable silence for a while until something caught Amanda's eye in the courtyard below.

"Look, there's a man with a Boston Terrier."

"Not so unusual," Fred commented, not looking up.

"But he's all bundled up with a rolled-up blanket on his back like a hobo. Do you think that could be the man we saw on the Common?"

Fred leaned forward for a closer look. "It could be. But we saw him from behind in the half-light so I couldn't be sure. He did have the same old-fashioned long coat on, though.'

"I remember that the dog's leash was red, but I can't see it from here."

"But look at him," Fred said. "It looks like a poor man's dog all wrapped up in rags."

He looked at her and dashed out of the room, down the stair and out to the courtyard as Amanda looked out the window. But the man below had finished his circuit of the area and by the time Fred got downstairs and then out to the street, the man had disappeared.

Chapter 8

Amanda got the evening paper before anyone else in the house and read the headline: "Building Director, Patrick Harris Killed." She sat down in an armchair without taking off her coat and pored over the dramatically written article. She stopped for a moment to see if there was a byline and her heart pounded as she relived the incident of finding the body near the bushes. Her father was not fond of the evening paper, thinking it focused excessively on local matters and crime, but her mother, an avid subscriber, would likely read it and once again open the conversation of 'good' and 'bad' parts of town. That would naturally lead to questioning Amanda's interest in working that would take them down the familiar path of settling down.

The reporter wrote that Harris had been 'viciously gunned down' which made it sound like a gangland killing, hardly a likely explanation for what had occurred. That made her wonder if he had been the victim of a robbery—she wanted to pick up the telephone and ask Detective

Halloran personally if that was the case, but she had inserted herself enough into the matter as it was. But surely the man hadn't walked all the way from Brookline with his dog? That meant that he must have driven to the Common. But why?

She was thinking this over and chewing on her thumb in concentration when the front bell rang, and the sudden sound almost made her jump out of the chair. Mary came out from the back of the house and answered the door, bringing Detective Halloran into the room, saying he was there to speak to her.

"I'm sorry, were you about to go out?" he asked. She folded the paper and put it face down on the table to her side and shook her head.

"Did you see this?" she asked, pointing to it.

"Oh, yes. That reporter likes to turn up the heat on any story he is assigned."

"Well, it is a shocking incident. But why have you come?"

"Had you ever met the man before?"

"The reporter or Patrick Harris?"

"The deceased."

"Certainly not." She picked up the paper and looked at the photograph of the man. To her eyes, it seemed no different than any other civil servant's official picture.

She looked up at Halloran and wondered why he had come all this way just to ask her that question but instead took the initiative to quiz him about the progress of the case.

"I was thinking that he must have driven to some place near the Common and then walked in. Has anybody found his car?"

Halloran gave a tight smile. "Good thinking. And no, we haven't found his car yet, but the description of a black, late model Ford that his wife gave us wasn't very helpful. She was so distressed she couldn't even remember the license plate number."

"Who takes note of their license plate number? It's attached to the car—all you have to do is get out and look."

He blinked in confusion.

"Why try to remember things when they are right in front of your face if you need to know it?"

"That's a good point. Do you know if Doctor Browne knew the man?"

Amanda was shocked at the question. "No, I don't know. But if he had ever met him or had him as a patient, you'd think he would have said something."

"Such as?"

"When he looked at the body, he would have said, 'It's Mr. Harris.' Not, 'someone's been shot.' You can't possibly suspect Fred?"

He didn't respond.

"That makes no sense. I'm sure Fred doesn't own a gun. And we were at the concert together and then began to walk home. There was no opportunity for him to have done such a thing. And certainly no motive if he didn't even know him."

"Just checking. Thank you for your time."

She noticed he hadn't even taken off his hat or coat as she walked him to the front door.

Her father was coming up the steps and the two men put their hands to their hats and nodded although Mr. Burnside looked puzzled.

"Have I met that man before?" he asked when Halloran got into his car.

"He's the detective working on the case of the man who was shot."

Her father propelled her back into the house and while taking off his coat asked her, "Why was he talking to you? You gave him all the information he could have needed already."

"I know, Daddy. I don't know why he is poking around. He even asked if Fred knew the man."

"Did he?"

"I don't know," Amanda answered, her voice rising as she wondered if he could have been one of Fred's patients. How else would they have known each other? "I need to freshen up before dinner," she said, making her way to the stairs.

Amanda was not looking forward to the dinner conversation which would circle back to the murder. She could pretend not to feel well, but then her mother would ask what the matter was, imagining that recent events were overwhelming. Added to that, she was hungry even after the filling lunch with Fred, so she thought she would direct most of the conversation to Louisa, asking her about her classes, her plans for the weekend and other trivia as a distraction.

It worked for the most part, but she could see her mother glancing at her from time to time and knew that some sort of lecture might be coming her way. Louisa picked up the ball, so to speak, and chattered about her friends, some of whom would be going south to get out of the cold. She was hoping that her parents would suggest she join them, but they were not cooperative in that regard, and she pressed harder.

"Daisy said that the train fare to Georgia was reasonable and, of course, they would put me up and feed me for the two weeks." Her thoughts were of the lovely tan she hoped to acquire that she could show off at the club in the new dress with the low-cut back that her mother was unaware she had bought.

Mr. Burnside put his knife and fork down across his plate to indicate that he was finished and said, "Louisa, you are not going to Georgia with your friend. You are enrolled in classes and that should be your priority."

Louisa pouted and wondered if she should attempt to cry but realized his mind was made up and there was no use in pestering him.

NOW THAT HER parents were worried about both daughters, Amanda got up early the next day, intending to eat breakfast and get out of the house before anyone else was up and about. Better yet, she tiptoed down the back-stairs, surprising the cook who rarely saw her in the kitchen.

"Just want to grab a bite before I need to go."

"Would you like me to cook you something? Eggs?"

"No, I'll just grab this roll and some cheese."

The cook looked at her as if she were demented; the family was always served properly either in the morning room or the dining room depending upon the time of day.

Amanda made her way to the garage knowing that her exit would not be heard by her parents and safely sneaked out without being discovered. She parked her car in the lot behind the hospital and looked over at the construction site where the workers were standing around the fire warming their hands. There was commotion with raised voices, and she wondered if these sites were prone to that sort of activity or if it was the fault of the foreman who seemed to wield his position aggressively. From the safety and warmth of her car, she watched as most of the workers faced away from that day's altercation between the foreman and someone who was not dressed as a construction worker.

As before, there was a lot of shouting, but this time the fingers jabbed into the chest went both ways. Amanda wondered who the other person was who then shoved the foreman away and received a fist to his jaw in reaction. Amanda thought surely someone would break up the impending fight, but the other man merely picked himself off the ground and walked toward the hospital. She waited until he was in the building before going in herself. It was early but the hospital operated at all hours, so she was able to access the administrative floor, which still hadn't got its enhanced security, and found the man standing in the empty hallway looking around.

"Can I help you?" she asked, thinking he had pressed the button for the wrong floor and needed to see a doctor after that roundhouse punch that had also scraped the skin of his cheek.

"I'm looking for Mr. Barlow."

"Just a minute. I don't think he's in yet." She knew that he wasn't because his door was closed and trying the handle, she found it locked.

"What, bankers' hours here?"

"It's only eight-thirty. He'll be in at nine if you'd like to wait. Unless you need to see a doctor for...," she pointed at his face. He swiped his hand across his cheek and observed the blood but didn't seem particularly concerned, taking a handkerchief out of his pocket to wipe his hands.

"What's going on out there, do you know?" he asked her.

"Yes, they are renovating the children's clinic," she said.

"Hah! I'll be back at nine." He strode to the elevator and pushed the button. "Tell Mr. Barlow that Gleason will be back by then to ask some questions."

"Can you spell that please?"

He obliged, in a curt manner, while she jotted it down on a slip of paper from Miss Bailey's desk. The bell sounded, the doors opened, and he went in, pressing the button assertively and glaring at her.

It wasn't until he was gone, and she looked at the name on the paper that she recognized it as the person who had written the article about the death of Patrick Harris. She quickly pressed the elevator button in the mistaken belief that the doors might open, he would appear, and she could ask him what he wanted to know. Of course, he had gone down to the first floor, and she had to wait until it came back up. Stepping in, she hesitated and decided to see if Fred was on his rounds as doctors usually were early in the day. On the third floor, she asked the nurse at the reception desk if Doctor Browne was in and found out that he was, indeed, checking on patients but was expected to be finished by nine o'clock. Nothing to do but wait.

Rounds were usually done early in the morning before the doctor's office hours, surgery or patient visits began. The floor was a hive of activity, with doctors and nurses striding quickly into the private rooms or finally the ward where the less wealthy patients were housed. At last, Fred came out from a doorway with a clipboard in one hand jotting notes as he walked. He only slowed down as he approached the nurses' station, either instinctively from the brighter lighting or out of sheer habit. He looked up with surprise to see Amanda sitting in the nearby waiting area.

"What are you doing here?" he asked with a smile.

"I work upstairs, remember?" she said. "Come, sit down. I have something to ask you."

"Of course, but only for a few minutes." He turned his full attention on her face, which he could see was worried.

"Did you know Patrick Harris?"

Fred's head pulled back in surprise. "I suppose so. He was once a patient of mine."

"You never said."

Fred stammered before saying, "Nobody asked."

"Didn't you recognize him when we found him?"

"Of course not. It was dark and he was concealed by the bushes. I felt for a pulse but didn't see his face. Or if I had, I wouldn't have made the connection."

They held each other's gaze for a few moments before a nurse came up and interrupted the conversation.

"Excuse me, Doctor Browne, but *that* patient is asking for you again." Her face indicated that the person in question was not shy of demanding attention.

"I'm sorry, I have to go. We'll talk later, all right?"

Amanda nodded and wondered if Fred was being evasive or just busy and preoccupied. She went back up to the administrative floor which was now populated with the usual staff.

"I left that note for you," Amanda said, pointing to a slip of paper on Miss Bailey's desk.

"Thank you, but who or what is Gleason?"

"He's a reporter with the afternoon newspaper."

"Did he say what he wanted?"

"Just to talk to Mr. Barlow."

Miss Bailey got up, knocked on his door and delivered the message to her boss, who wrinkled his forehead wondering what could be of interest to the evening reader before putting it aside.

Amanda thought about telling him what she had observed and decided for the moment to let it go, regretting it within the hour when Gleason came storming back up to the administrative floor insisting on seeing Mr. Barlow.

Miss Bailey reeled back in alarm as they rarely had pugnacious visitors to their floor and the loud demands brought Amanda out of her office to see what the matter was.

"You!" he said pointing his finger at her. "Did you know about all this?"

"All this what?" she answered.

Mr. Barlow had emerged from his office when he heard the man's loud voice. "What—"

"Did you know that no permit had been issued for the construction out there?" Gleason jerked his thumb in the general direction of the rear of the hospital where work on the clinic was being done.

"Of course, there is a permit. We hired an architect to design it and a reputable construction company to do the work. What makes you think there isn't a permit."

"It is supposed to be clearly visible on site, usually nailed to the side of the building."

Mr. Barlow let out an exasperated sigh. "Perhaps it blew down in the wind or something. Come on, let's check. I'm Mr. Barlow, by the way," he said holding out his hand.

"Gleason," was the only answer and he shook the hand with a sharp jerk.

"Let me get my coat," Mr. Barlow said, retreating to his office and putting his arms through the sleeves as he came out. They went down the elevator in silence, Barlow maintaining a strained smile and Gleason scowling.

"Phew," Miss Bailey said. "What a hothead!"

"I guess you haven't seen many of his articles in the paper. All very bombastic with unfounded suppositions."

Miss Bailey gasped. "*That* Gleason! He was pestering my friend for information. Can you imagine? Her husband killed in such a shocking manner and this man is knocking on her door and calling on the phone to ask all sorts of insulting questions."

"Such as?"

"Were they happily married, did he have any gambling debts, did he associate with any known criminals, and so on."

"That's dreadful. Let's hope he doesn't make something up!" She shook her head and went back to work.

It wasn't too long after that Amanda once again heard voices in the reception area and poked her head out of her office to see what the matter was. She wasn't sure, but Mr. Barlow didn't look pleased, and Gleason had a nasty smirk on his face.

Chapter 9

What Gleason hadn't told Mr. Barlow before their on-site inspection was that he very well knew there was not a permit for the renovation of the clinic. He had already been to the Buildings Department and asked to see the original document in his usual belligerent manner, thoroughly intimidating the young woman behind the desk to search for what he wanted. When she had come back empty-handed, he had spun on his heel and left abruptly. Gleason knew that in the morass of bureaucratic paperwork, it might very well be there, but it made for a better story for that evening's edition to state that a 'preliminary search' turned up no documentation pertaining to the expensive renovation taking place. He was thinking how best to portray the ruffians at the site and the assault by the foreman without mentioning specifically that they were Italians. There were phrases he could use alluding to their lack of understanding of his request due to language incompatibility, which would get the point across to the readers without actually stating it.

"I'll call the architect right now and see that he follows up," Barlow said as Gleason made himself comfortable in the chair in the office. He glanced around at the expensive wooden cabinets with their glass fronts and the large window with a view of the Boston skyline. Barlow did not miss the appraising looks of the reporter and since the architect was on another site, proposed that they both go to the Buildings Department and find the document which he knew had to be there.

Gleason was surprised by the suggestion and agreed although he felt a slight hesitation: it was possible that the young woman who had helped him was so flustered that she didn't do a thorough enough search. She was still on duty behind the front desk when the two men entered later, and she said she would locate her supervisor, more than glad not to have to deal with Gleason, whose eyes were already narrowed in distrust.

A man came out and introduced himself as the manager of the division and said he would get the Deputy Director immediately to see to the issue. He ushered them into a small conference room, and they waited, coats folded over the back of the chairs until another man entered the room followed by the manager they had previously met.

"Ron King," he announced with a broad smile, holding his hand out to Mr. Barlow, whom he wasn't sure if he had met before. He was well aware of who Gleason was and gave him a nod of his head with its slicked back, dark brown hair. "Deputy Director," he clarified. "What can I do for you?"

"We're looking for the building permit for the Mercy Hospital Children's Clinic," Gleason said before Mr. Barlow could respond.

"We should be able to find that for you. Who are the architects who did the design? That might be the easiest way to find it. Or how recently did work begin?"

Barlow supplied the information and King snapped his fingers at the manager who walked away quickly down the hall while the three men remained in the room.

"Terrible thing about Mr. Harris," Barlow said.

"I'll say. It seems the criminal element is everywhere in this city now. Can't take a stroll without being attacked. Do you know if the police have any information about who did this?"

Gleason spoke up, "From what I learned, he was shot and then dragged off the path. Whoever did it supposed that no one would find the body until the morning, if that."

"Did they find a weapon?"

"No, they didn't. It's likely at the bottom of the bay. That's what thugs do with their cheap guns when they're done with them," Gleason said.

King looked down at his fingers and wiped at a dried smudge of ink from his middle finger. He smoothed his hair down and said, "We'll find that permit. Never fear."

Gleason snorted and they sat in silence for some time before the manager came back.

The manager looked at King from the doorway; he then exited, closing the door to the hall behind them so they could confer quietly.

"Doesn't look good," Gleason said with a slight smirk.

"That's impossible," Barlow responded.

After a few minutes, King came back into the room and without sitting down said, "There must be some irregularity in the filing. I seem to remember I signed off on it, now that you have mentioned the architects, and then it would have gone to Mr. Harris for his signature. Then, back down to the records division where the actual permit would have been stamped and issued."

"So, you can't locate the application?"

"I'm afraid at this time I cannot," King said.

"Can we look for it?" Gleason asked.

"What? You mean rummage around in the files? Absolutely not. First, the file room is an historical record of construction in the city of Boston. We can't have the public rifling through those documents, possibly misfiling or pilfering something. We have staff here and we will continue to search. I'm confident it is somewhere in the building." His stance, angled away from the doorway, seemed to indicate that the discussion was over, but Gleason wasn't having it.

"Can we take a look at the Director's office?

King was taken aback. "The police looked it over, although what they thought they would find, I don't know."

"Well, can we?"

King hesitated and knowing that any reluctance to cooperate would show up in the next day's evening paper—or perhaps that evening's paper—if Gleason were quick to file his copy.

"Yes, I suppose so. It's just a normal office."

When they got up to the next floor, which consisted of an open room with many desks, all eyes were on them. King led them to a corner office that didn't look like any workplace that Barlow or Gleason had ever seen. There were shelves of files lying on their side in a bookcase behind the desk and the wall was covered in signed photographs of boxers in the usual stance facing the camera looking ferocious. A woman came into view in the doorway and watched the activity with concern.

"Quite a sports fan, huh?" Gleason commented.

King shrugged.

Gleason walked closer as if to inspect the signature of the fighter while flicking his finger on the topmost file to see what was there. At that moment, King reached out his hand to stop any further snooping and in doing so, knocked the file onto the floor.

"Look what you've done!" King said before stooping to pick up one sheet after another.

"Those look like applications to me," Gleason said.

"Yes, I signed them. You can see that."

"And he didn't?" Barlow asked.

King went on his knees and retrieved several papers. "I signed these over two weeks ago."

Gleason shuffled through the papers on the floor. "Look at how many there are. I'll bet yours is among them," he said, looking at Barlow.

Suddenly, it was a cooperative environment where they read out the names of projects to one another as they came across them.

"Here you are," Gleason said, showing Barlow what they had come looking for.

"This is a travesty," Barlow said. "How are you going to fix this?"

"I'll talk to the Mayor right away and see how we can get things moving again." Turning to Gleason he said, "I would appreciate it if you didn't write about this."

It was met with a laugh from the reporter. "You think if you say 'pretty please' I'll keep this information from the public? Taxpayers' money wasted, commerce interrupted, ineptitude at the top in the Buildings Department? Not on your life." He stormed out of the office, forcing the woman who stood there to move aside.

"He is probably composing the article as he walks back to his office," King said. "Do you need something, Miss Jones?" he asked curtly.

She stammered before saying, "His office didn't usually look like that."

"The police probably left it like this." King pushed past her. "Excuse me, I'd better go to the Mayor's office in person," and he took off down the hallway, leaving the shocked manager and Barlow to look down on the mess of papers on the floor.

"I'll get somebody to sort this out," she said, kneeling to shuffle through the remaining papers.

"Make sure whoever it is doesn't lose track of my application again." Barlow shook his head in frustration and wondered what to tell the construction company. Would they have to send the men home until this was rectified?

Who knew how long that could take—days, weeks? How could this level of bad management have been going on without somebody's noticing?

Chapter 10

Things moved quickly after the discovery of the disaster of the late Patrick Harris' office with a furious Mayor immediately appointing Ron King as Director with the caveat to 'clean it up fast.' King said he would be glad to do so, but hesitated at the salary that his former boss had made, which resulted in a hefty raise for the new man along with further expletive-laden comments from the Mayor, whether directed at Harris for creating the situation or King to get moving on the issue that was about to hit the newspapers.

It wasn't even five o'clock when Barlow had Miss Bailey run out to the newsstand at the busy corner where the foot traffic was heavy and bring back a copy of the evening newspaper.

He was shocked at how quickly the reporter had managed to write the story even if it was short on facts and long on hyperbole, and he fully expected that by morning most of the Board members would be calling to find out what this meant for the renovation of the clinic. To his great relief, Ron King called him almost immediately and stated that he had been appointed Director and, as such, would be signing off on the application as soon as possible.

"You'll get it if I have to walk it through the last division that needs to affix its stamp on the paper."

"Thank you, Mr. King."

"And let me apologize again for any trouble this has caused you."

"Apology accepted," Barlow replied, and they ended the conversation.

Miss Bailey appeared in the doorway with her coat on, an expectant look on her face.

"All is well," he said.

She sighed in relief. "I'm so glad. But I just can't believe Patrick Harris could have allowed that to happen in the first place. He seemed like such a conscientious person." She seemed about to say something else but ended with a curt goodnight.

AMANDA HAD BEEN HOME for some time and was reading the explosive article in the evening newspaper when her mother came into the sitting room.

"I thought you and your father didn't approve of that paper," she said with raised eyebrows.

"Mother, that might be Daddy's opinion, but this reporter has captured my attention because of his energy, not his outrageous output. I can't believe that Mr. Harris' family won't sue the paper for the almost libelous comments."

"My view exactly," her father said, coming in the front door through the vestibule.

"Have you read it already?"

"It's the talk of the city. I heard the Mayor was furious as he thinks anything that reflects badly on one of his Irish cronies will stick to him." He sat down in an armchair and said, "Good evening, dear," to his wife.

"I thought we were all done with this business of distrusting the Mayor because of his Irish roots," Amanda said.

"It's not where his family comes from that matters to me. It's how he operates the power that has been vested in him. Giving favors and appointments to those who backed him and raised money for his election rather than professionals who might know what they're doing. I'm sure that's how this entire situation developed," he said.

"I don't know anything about the matter, but one must feel sympathy for the family of the poor man who died. Not only must it have been a great shock, but now his name is being dragged through the mud. With no one to defend him," Mrs. Burnside said, taking the paper from Amanda and tut-tutting as she read the article about him.

"You can be sure the Mayor will wash his hands of the man. And I had heard he was going to attend the funeral tomorrow and speak about the loyal employee who had been gunned down so that he could emphasize the need to crack down on crime. I don't imagine he will make an appearance now, considering the circumstances."

"Well, I'm going," Amanda said. Her parents stared at her.

"Do you think that's a good idea?" He mother asked. "It might bring back dreadful memories of discovering his body in the first place. And your presence could upset his family, as well."

"I'm giving Miss Bailey a ride to the Mass and the interment afterward. She was hesitant to ask Mr. Barlow for time off for the entire event—."

"And don't they usually have some kind of feast after the burial?" her mother asked. "With a lot of drinking?"

"I couldn't say, Mother. I will keep well away from the family although I'm sure they don't know who I am or what connection I have with them. If she attends, whatever occurs afterwards, that's her business."

Her mother shook her head. "I don't understand some of these odd customs," she concluded.

Amanda remembered the funeral of her grandmother and how solemn and restrained everyone was. That was what was expected in her family, and they seemed to have little patience for the more effusive expressions of the other cultures who had come to live in Boston. She thought it was such an outdated attitude considering immigrants had been settling in the area for centuries, including her own family long ago.

The conversation stopped as Nora came into the room to relay the news that Louisa had called and would not be dining with them that evening. The message, once delivered, resulted in the senior Burnsides looking at each other in astonishment.

"I've been home for hours. Why didn't she tell me? Why call and leave a message with the maid?"

They looked at Amanda for an explanation, but she just shrugged and said, "I have no idea." But of course, she had a very good idea where Louisa was and why she had not spoken to her mother directly.

THE NEXT MORNING, Amanda let Mr. Barlow know that she was transporting Miss Bailey to Patrick Harris' funeral, but he hardly heard her as he was preoccupied with calling the Board members to alert them to what had happened. She suggested to Miss Bailey that they leave early in the event there was a crowd. As she had expected, there was almost nowhere to park in the immediate vicinity of the Cathedral of the Holy Cross, but she managed to find what appeared to be a space on a nearby side street.

The line of people waiting to get into the church snaked out onto the street and, although a crowd in mourning, there was an undertone of anger likely from the unfavorable depiction of Mr. Harris in the previous day's newspaper. There was muttering as people walked up the impressive exterior stairs and glances back over shoulders as if expecting the reporter himself to show up—not that any knew what he looked like.

Amanda, brought up in the Episcopal church, or Anglican, as her mother often referred to it, had never set foot in the Cathedral of the Holy Cross and was amazed at its size and splendor, having expected it to be more ordinary. Amanda hadn't been to a Catholic Mass before and wished to stay anonymously toward the back of the massive crowd, but Miss Bailey, who considered herself close to the family, walked toward the front and Amanda had no choice but to follow. They squeezed into a pew next to someone Miss Bailey smiled at and attempted an introduction to Amanda, but the name was lost in the whispered tone of voice.

It was surprisingly noisy as more people shuffled in and an organ began to play. Amanda looked around at the stained-glass windows and the swooping Gothic arches that defined the nave and the aisles. Perhaps the first Catholic immigrants has been satisfied with a less impressive structure, but this replacement 'rivaled both Old South Church and Trinity Church in grandeur' she read from the small brochure in the wooden pocket of the pew before them. By the time the new cathedral was built, it was a more prosperous population that was served. Amanda knew she was gaping a bit and as her gaze returned to the parishioners, Detective Halloran caught her eye and lifted one corner of his mouth in recognition.

Her immediate reaction was: what was he doing there? Then, as she gave it more thought, of course, he would be in attendance, possibly to observe who might be guilty—at least that's what she read the police did. However, he may have known or interacted with Mr. Harris in a professional situation and that would explain his presence. She looked back at him, and his calm demeanor suggested that he was there to observe, but she planned to keep an eye on him to see to whom he spoke when the service was over.

The organ stopped playing and the priest and two attendants came out. Everyone stood and Amanda made sure to mirror the actions of the others, which involved kneeling, standing and at one point sitting. It was confusing to her, and she expected that the priest would give a sermon, but he continued with the ritual up to a portion where the host was raised, and everyone murmured. With the tinkling of chimes and the further responses, people began to get up and get in two lines in the aisles. For a moment, Amanda thought she was supposed to follow, but Miss Bailey shook her head subtly and she came to realize that those standing were about to receive Communion.

There were dozens of people who partook after the family had taken the host and she surreptitiously glanced at the watch on her wrist and wondered when this would ever end. It did mark the culmination of the most important part of the service, and after more standing and kneeling, the Mass seemed to be over. There was an orderly exit of the rows of pews starting with the family, the heavily veiled widow half-bent with grief and supported by a man's arm, then row by row, the Cathedral emptied out onto the steps and plaza in front.

"Now we'll go to the interment," Miss Bailey said. "Do you know the way?"

While the Mass had been an interesting experience, Amanda dreaded going to the cemetery although there would not be as many people present. She was correct, but it was still a horde of people, and she wondered how Mrs. Harris could endure this endless ceremony of grief that might be followed by a luncheon of some sort. Somehow in the mass of people, Miss Bailey was able to approach her friend, put her hand on her arm and express her condolences, probably not for the first time.

"How can you bear to work at that dreadful hospital," Mrs. Harris said, pulling away. After all they've done to Patrick."

Miss Bailey looked shocked before both women turned away from each other and she staggered into Amanda on the uneven ground.

"We'd better go," Miss Bailey said.

They walked back through the crowd that was assembling to Amanda's car parked some distance away and she could see Miss Bailey was crying. Nearby was an empty side path with a large weeping willow, now devoid of leaves, and a stone bench that Amanda drew Miss Bailey toward to sit down.

"What was that about?"

Miss Bailey sighed. "She's never forgiven me for taking the job at Mercy Hospital. I didn't know at the time that Patrick had been hospitalized there once and developed a serious infection. They blamed the doctor and the hospital and wanted to sue but were persuaded by others in the family to drop the idea once he was well. It took him a long time to recover, and he wanted the incident behind him, but my friend was bitter about it, claiming it almost cost him his job."

"I can understand now that he's gone, she may want to blame others for what happened, but I don't see what the hospital has got to do with this situation."

"Neither do I," Miss Bailey said. She looked over Amanda's shoulder and said, "Oh," holding a gloved hand to her mouth.

Amanda turned and saw that Detective Halloran was approaching, having come late.

"Good morning, ladies," he said, tipping his hat. "May I help with something?" he asked, noticing Miss Bailey fishing for a handkerchief in her handbag.

"It's just an upsetting event," Amanda said.

"Excuse me, Brendan," Miss Bailey said, walking a short distance away to compose herself and discreetly blow her nose.

"Was Mrs. Harris on her about the hospital incident?"

"Why, yes. How did you know?"

"I heard from someone that Mrs. Harris wanted to press charges, but was told it was a civil matter, not criminal and to leave it alone."

"And did they?"

"Leave it alone? I'm not sure. Someone seemed hell-bent on destroying Doctor Browne's reputation. Good day." He tipped his hat, leaving Amanda staring at his retreating form, more disturbed than she could imagine.

Chapter 11

"I think we ought to return to the office, don't you?" Amanda asked, having no intention of injecting herself into the family's post-funeral luncheon and now certain that Miss Bailey would not be welcome. She looked over at the distressed young woman as they pulled out into traffic.

"I didn't know that you knew Detective Halloran," Amanda said.

"Brendan? Yes, he and my older brother went to school together. John chose to be a fireman and Brendan went into the police force. They used to joke that between them they had the city covered." She managed a small smile. "My brother is an Assistant Captain, so he fared better than his friend."

"What do mean by that? Isn't Detective a good position?" Amanda was trying to concentrate on driving through increasingly heavy traffic yet interested in more information about him.

"It's good enough, I suppose, although John said he might not go further. The police chief doesn't like him."

"Why not?"

"He went to Boys Latin and then Boston University."

"What? Don't they want educated people on the police force?"

"Too big for his britches is the attitude. At least from the police chief."

"How do you know that? Don't tell me. Someone else in your family is in the police department," Amanda said.

"Why yes, how did you know?" Miss Bailey said in all seriousness.

She dropped Miss Bailey off at the hospital to go join the X-Ds for their monthly lunch at Valerie's club where they could have a private dining room for what she called their 'gabfest.'

She and Amanda had been friends since childhood, attended the same schools, gone to the same parties and 'come out' at the same time in the hotel where Louisa later had her debut. Since it was January, several of the girls were not in attendance, some spending a few weeks in Florida, Patricia on a cruise with her mother and Veronica in Arizona, of all places. It was just six of them that day and as Amanda was the last to arrive, dressed all in black, her friends looked at her in alarm.

"Is there…?" Marnie asked.

"I had to attend a funeral."

"I'm so sorry," Gayle said, looking concerned and pulling her gloves off finger by finger.

"I hadn't heard…," Marnie pursued.

"I accompanied someone with whom I work." Amanda knew that mentioning the word 'work' would engender many questions, so she amended her answer. "Where I've been volunteering at the hospital. Someone was too upset to go by herself and, frankly, didn't have any transportation, so I ended up going with her."

"I hate funerals," Cecile said. She sipped her water and looked around the table for confirmation from her friends.

"I don't suppose anyone enjoys them," Amanda said.

"But that *is* a lovely suit," Betsy commented.

"Thank you," Amanda said, thinking it fit her exceptionally well.

Two waiters came in and put a small glass of tomato juice at each place setting and left without a word.

"Chin chin, girls," Valerie said. "To the X-Ds."

They raised their glasses, smiled at one another and took a sip.

"I somehow feel we should have created a special handshake or motto, like the fraternities have."

"X-Ds sounds like some spy group," Cecile said.

"Or an invisible ray that keeps us forever young."

"Let's call ourselves a Tribe of Something-or-other."

Amanda didn't respond but realized that they were indeed a tribe. Of rich young women, mostly single, entirely focused on not being single for long and all waiting for something exciting to happen to them. Mostly they were waiting for love or marriage, but she still couldn't put her finger on what she was waiting for except something with purpose.

Sensing her quiet mood, Gayle asked, "Amanda, was it terribly sad?"

"I might as well tell the whole story," she said. "It was the funeral for the man who was found shot on Boston Common. The man who Fred Browne and I came upon as we walked through one night."

The room was silent then raucous with demands for more information and scolding remarks that she hadn't informed any of them of the event until just then.

"I think I saw something about it in the newspaper although my mother tends to keep me away from reading the sordid stories. They didn't mention your name, did they?" Marnie asked.

"No, thank goodness. That would have sent my parents over the edge. It was bad enough that it happened, but I was with Fred—"

"Oh, dear," someone said.

"Yes, they were not best pleased that he had walked me through the Common in the first place."

"Doesn't he have a car?"

"Of course," Amanda said irritably. "But we had walked over to the concert in the early afternoon because the weather wasn't so bad and, I don't know, it didn't seem so odd then to walk back home." The girls looked at one another and then down at their empty place settings.

It fell to the newly engaged Betsy to impart some wisdom to the conversation. "I feel it is important that one's boyfriend or fiancé always offer protection. Not just to physical harm but to social comments or gossip. I hope he hasn't exposed you to remarks about the incident."

Amanda thought she sounded like a middle-aged mother, not a young woman in her early twenties. Was this her tribe? Censorious, wealthy young women with standards to which one must adhere?

The two waiters came back in with large serving trays that they placed on the sideboard and then transferred a plate of lettuce, chicken salad, and fruit in front of each guest.

"Thank you, Valerie. I love the crab salad here, but I'm glad you chose the chicken. I'm modeling this afternoon and I didn't want to smell like fish." Marnie giggled. "I probably should only have a bite anyway; I absolutely need to fit into the divine dress that I'll be showing off."

"Do you enjoy that work?" Amanda asked.

"It's hardly work. I get to try on lovely garments and Monsieur Josef provides a woman who does our hair and makeup."

"That does sound wonderful," Valerie said.

"I get paid, but it's fun to be a bit of a showoff from time to time."

"Only time to time?" Cecile asked, softening her remark with a smile.

"Emerson said he saw you at the hospital," Valerie said to Amanda.

"That's right," Amanda said. She looked down at her meager lunch, accompanied by melba toast for some reason, which this club served the ladies. "He seemed in good spirits about his job."

Valerie gave a happy exhalation. "He seems to have found something he really likes."

"What now?" Cecile asked.

"He's working for an architectural firm drafting and so on. I think he'll stick with it this time." Everyone smiled indulgently at Valerie's optimism since he seemed to have previously tried several professions without luck.

"What are you still doing at the hospital?" Marnie asked Amanda.

"I was doing administrative tasks, but the new director asked me to make suggestions as to the design of the children's clinic renovation."

"That sounds interesting," Betsy said. "Gosh, I forgot to show up this week."

"Maybe Amanda can help you decorate your new home," Cecile said.

"What a wonderful idea!" Betsy said.

"I think Cecile was pulling your leg. I don't know more than any of you about interior design. I just observed the crowded and impersonal former reception area, talked to a few of the mothers who were waiting and came up with ideas to make it less institutional."

"It was rather bleak last year staring at the light green walls," Valerie said, remembering her lengthy stay with at the hospital as a patient, although not in the clinic. "But the staff were really nice."

"What's Louisa up to?" Gayle asked.

"Oh, my gosh!" Amanda looked at her watch, having lost track of time. "Right now, she is standing on a street corner waiting for her older sister to pick her up. Got to go! Next time!" She hurried out to the cloakroom to get her coat and raced to the street to get into her car.

"She's going to kill me," she said aloud, speeding down the street toward the school which was not too far from the club. It was the usual gray, windy, January day and Louisa would be in a cranky mood after having to wait outside.

It was less than ten minutes later that Amanda pulled up to the front of the school where Louisa was the only person waiting at the foot of the steps, her shoulders hunched into her coat.

"Where've you been?" she said as she got into the car. "I'm frozen."

"Sorry, I'll turn up the heat. Are you the last person here? I'm not that late."

Louisa merely gave her sister a sidelong glance. They stopped at a red light and saw Detective Halloran in the car beside them. He rolled down his window and flashed a smile.

"So, we meet again."

"Indeed," Amanda said, wondering if the man were following her.

"No, I meant both of you."

The light changed and he went ahead while Amanda looked at Louisa who was fiddling with her gloves.

"What did he mean by that?" Amanda asked.

The car behind honked its horn and she drove on.

"Really, what did he mean?"

"I can't imagine."

Amanda pulled over but kept the engine running. "I mean it. What's going on? Are you now going to classes? If so, where did he see you recently?"

"Oh, all right!" Louisa said. "I had lunch with Rob today."

Amanda stared.

"That's all. At a restaurant, not at his club, as you may have thought."

"No, I guess the club is for your evening rendezvous."

"Don't be such a prig, Amanda. "Just because your boyfriend is a stuffy doctor—"

"He's not stuffy."

"When is the last time you went out to a club with him? Or dancing?"

Amanda thought back to the group of people whom he knew that enjoyed Early Music concerts and could talk effortlessly about instruments of which she had never heard. She signaled and pulled back out into traffic without responding. They drove in silence all the way to Beacon Hill where Amanda stopped in front of their door.

"I have to go back to the hospital for an hour or two. Don't get into any trouble while I'm gone," she said as her sister got out of the car.

"I know you won't," Louisa shot back at her.

Amanda thought it was a good thing that she didn't have a regular job since she had spent more than half the day doing other things. No wonder the X-Ds didn't work; there was no time for work with lunches and shopping and preparing for the next engagement party or wedding. Not for the first time she wished her parents weren't so conservative about money. They had plenty, that wasn't the issue, but she longed to be able to go somewhere warm for a vacation in the winter. Just once.

She parked her car and saw the familiar sight of the workmen surrounding the fire and wondered if some of them ever did anything besides try to keep themselves warm. It had to be a difficult life, finding work in the first place, then working in all kinds of weather—cold, snow, rain and the stifling humidity in the summers. How did anyone break out of that pattern of manual labor if you couldn't save enough to learn to do anything else? She compared the life of those men she saw each day with Emerson's, where he would try one kind of job, decide he didn't like it and then through family or school contacts, start something else. In the midst of the Depression, no less.

Mr. Barlow was in an unusually bad mood when she came out of the elevator and brusquely asked her where she had been. He had never spoken to her like that before and a look at Miss Bailey's puffy eyes told her that he had probably barked at her as well.

"I attended the funeral of Mr. Harris this morning and then had to drive my sister back from school. I hope I haven't upset your schedule," she said, realizing it sounded condescending, but she was not going to put up with being treated in such a manner. Miss Bailey tried to hide a smile although Mr. Barlow wasn't looking in her direction.

"Excuse me. I'm a bit overwhelmed by events. Please come into my office."

Amanda took off her coat, looked at Miss Bailey for a clue as to what was going on and got a shrug in response.

"Just to update you, we still haven't got the permit. Then Mr. Romano informs me that due to the delays and the rising costs of materials, there has been a cost overrun."

"What does that mean?"

"It means that although he made a bid for the job and we accepted it, now he is submitting bills for additional funds so the project will cost more."

"But how could there have been delays when they shouldn't have been working in the first place? And pardon me for saying so, but every time I've been over at the clinic to see what work has been done, it looks exactly the same."

"As you know, I am too busy to be checking on things over there on a regular basis, but I can't help but agree with you from what I've seen. They did some demolition and put up some temporary interior walls but that seems to be the extent of what's been done."

"If they haven't done much, how can they request funds for an increase in the cost of materials?"

"As you might guess, in these times especially, the suppliers want to be paid ahead of delivery. Not one hundred per cent, but perhaps half. Because they don't know when Romano is going to be reimbursed for the completed work and they have to carry those costs."

Mr. Barlow sighed. "They had better do a damned good job on the clinic because it must pass inspection. And if it doesn't, Romano won't get paid until it does. And he won't pay his suppliers until he has the cash in hand. I didn't like accepting his bid in the first place, having heard some gossip about his business practices, but it was the lowest bid, so the Board felt obligated. Now I feel as if he is playing us and trying to gouge us financially."

"And what about the suppliers and the workmen? Could he decide not to pay them, too?"

"I'm not sure. But I don't like how this is going at all."

Chapter 12

Giving it a bit more thought, Amanda wondered if keeping the temporary clinic location in the main building wasn't the solution to the financial issues with the contractor and a way to get out of the mess with the permit. And how could the contractor expect to get paid if there was no permit in place? He shouldn't have been allowed to do any of the demolition much less construction —if you could call it that—to begin with.

She went down to the bustling first floor and then to the clinic's entrance, which was easy to spot from the number of women and children coming and going. The reception area was packed but every woman had a seat, even if her child did not. That's what laps were for. The tight quarters did not seem to bother any of them, rather the opposite. They acted as if they were in this curious situation together and might as well make the best of it with talking and laughter. Her presence wasn't noticed until one little boy came crashing into her legs as he raced around the room.

"I'm sorry, Miss," the mother said. Amanda thought she must look very official and severe in her black suit, so she smiled and reassured her that nothing was damaged. As she looked around the room, she wondered how far these women had to travel to get to the hospital and how many more children were at home. This might be an entire day's excursion with a sick child, which could mean other chores at home were waiting, something she had thought about before, but now she wondered how these women accomplished all they must have to do in a day.

"Miss, I heard that the clinic building might not get finished anytime soon," one woman asked her.

"Oh, where did you hear that?" Amanda asked, affecting a surprised expression.

"My man works in the trades and one of his Hibernian brothers who works in the Buildings Department told him of it."

"As far as I know, it's still happening. Just a slowdown because of the weather, I expect."

The woman nodded, knowing that while working out of doors in the Boston winter was difficult at best, work still got done.

Retreating to the administrative floor, Amanda asked Mr. Barlow if she could have a few more minutes of his time. She reported what she had witnessed in the clinic and suggested they abandon renovation of the former location and just bring it into the hospital proper.

He raised his eyebrows and took a deep breath. "I appreciate your putting your mind to help solve this problem of cost, but we can't just cancel the project now."

"Why not?"

"We signed a contract. If we try to back out of it, Romano will certainly sue, as would be his legal right. He presumably has debts from paying the workers and ordering materials although he hasn't billed us yet and he'd be entitled to that reimbursement."

"It can't be that much. You've seen the site and it doesn't look like much has happened. People come and go into the building but mostly they stand around trying to keep warm and getting yelled at by the foreman."

Barlow chuckled at that description. "But we have a contract and there is a standard clause which requires the contractor and/or the hospital to inform the other party if there are some impediments that could affect the completion of the project. In other words, I can't just say we don't want to do the project anymore."

"Even though there has been no permit issued for it?"

"Good point. But we've already incurred costs with the architect and legal fees, so it is best we follow the original plan."

Amanda bit her lip in thought. "I'm not trying to sabotage the project, Mr. Barlow. It's just that every time I go down to the clinic reception area, it occurs to me that the mothers may seem cheerful enough under the circumstances of having a sick child, but they come here from all over the city, and wouldn't it be more convenient to have small clinics out in the neighborhoods? Perhaps not open every day as we are here, but certain days of the week."

"Interesting idea. There is the problem of finding space for something and then paying for it, as well as then assigning a doctor to travel from one location to another depending upon the day."

"There are already two doctors on duty each day in the clinic. One of them could be the roving doctor and perhaps have residents assist him. I bet if we look at the registration information of the patients in the clinic, we can figure out what neighborhoods they are from."

Barlow looked at her with renewed interest. "What a fascinating idea. Would you consider taking on that task now that the design function is largely done on paper and on hold in actuality?"

"Yes, I would be happy to do that. Thank you." Amanda got up and shook Mr. Barlow's hand, feeling very capable, competent and professional. It seemed she had managed to work herself into an actual job. Of some sort.

AMANDA AND FRED were to have dinner at his mother's house that evening, an event that she alternatively considered with anticipation and dread. Her family knew the Brownes, of course, being longtime residents of Beacon Hill, but she had not had much interaction with Fred's parents, his father having died before she got to know him, and his mother such an odd creature. Amanda's cousin, Aggie, had spent a weekend at Browne's Castle, their country house in Vermont the previous winter and was almost hesitant to give any details about the family knowing that Fred had come more closely into her orbit.

What Amanda knew was that Fred's father had been a successful businessman with international interests and his wife, Hextilda, being left alone for long periods began a hobby that developed into a career. She wrote historical romance novels, what some people called 'bodice rippers,' due to the steamy situations that the heroine found herself in. Except that Hextilda focused her attention on a male main character, Alistair, who was a fugitive from the English authorities, suffering land grabs, personal humiliations, but always coming out on top. And his loyal girlfriend, who became his wife in one of the many novels in the series, stuck by him through thick and thin while also being harassed by the English. The books sold like hotcakes and Hextilda developed the author persona of an eccentric, which allowed her to say outrageous things that she hadn't been able to express previously.

With such a parent, it was strange that Fred was such a buttoned-up person, very structured in his approach to life where his mother chose to break the rules; patient and directed where his mother was dramatic and erratic; opposites in every way. Fred's sister, Caroline, had been more interested in artistic endeavors and combined with her father's entrepreneurial bent had a gallery in Manhattan featuring the more avant-garde artists. While it thrived during the late 1920s, the Crash had a devastating effect on the art market, and she was forced to close it down. However, she had met and married José Pérez de Guzmán, a charming Latin American whose father had been in the consular service before losing that position due to a regime change. The Browne home in Beacon Hill housed mother, son, daughter and son-in-law in a seemingly harmonious household. Still, Hextilda liked to play games, especially with peoples' expectations, and Amanda was never sure what to expect from an evening at their home.

Fred came to pick her up promptly, as he was always on time, and gave her a kiss on the cheek. Amanda wondered if he had ever read any of his mother's books, where the hero was much bolder in his greeting of the woman in whom he was interested.

"I've brought the car, which seems silly since we're just a few blocks away, but it is warmer than walking in the cold and I feared you might have a bad association about 'taking a walk' with Fred."

"Nonsense," Amanda said, being helped into her coat. "But I do appreciate the car's heater. And men don't seem to realize that it is not always comfortable to wear heels all day long and walk what seems miles in them."

"Perhaps someday, women will realize they don't have to go to such extremes," Fred said.

Amanda glanced down at her elegant suede shoes and knew there was no way she would trade them in for something more utilitarian unless they were tramping through the woods on a hike. Another unlikely activity.

The Brownes' house was laid out much like her own except the furnishings were more ostentatious, as befitted the owner's personality. Hextilda was seated closest to the fire, the light shining on youthful brown hair although the lines on her face were a better indicator of her real age. In the Burnsides' old-fashioned sense of the world, older women did not dye their hair—that was something actresses or performers did to prolong their careers. Perhaps that was Hextilda's reasoning; she had been writing the same sort of novels for years and was trying to preserve her looks to match the photo that she continued to use on the back flap of each new release.

"Hello, my dear," she greeted Amanda, not getting up but extending her hand to draw the younger woman closer for a brief kiss on the cheek. "Don't you look charming this evening. As always, that's what Frederick says."

He looked puzzled as if trying to remember when he said those exact words or wondering if it was just his mother writing dialogue for him.

"Do pour us some sherry," she said to her son.

Hextilda kept the house warm, another clue that she might not be a proper Yankee who tended to be thrifty even if there was plenty of money.

Fred filled the cordial glasses with sherry and brought them over then retrieved one for himself before sitting down. "Where's Caroline?"

"Primping, likely. I've never known her to be satisfied with what she has first chosen to wear. There is the endless changing and then coordinating jewelry. And she never hangs up what she has discarded. The poor maids spend more time tidying her room than all the rest of the bedrooms."

"Mother, why do you allow her to behave that way? It's so irresponsible. I can't imagine what her apartment in New York must have looked like with no one to pick up after her."

"I don't have to imagine. I saw it first-hand. It looked like a bomb had gone off!" She laughed all the same. "I thought when she got married, she would become more thoughtful or organized."

"Really, Mother. She's always been like that. I can't imagine how she ran a business. That's probably why it didn't work out."

"That's not why it didn't work out and you know it, Mr. Stuffy," said Caroline, who had silently come from behind his chair and flicked him on the back of the head with her long red nails. "Hello, you," she greeted Amanda in the usual way.

She dramatically perched on the edge of the sofa, crossed her silk stockinged legs and looked at Fred in expectation, raising her thin eyebrows in expectation that he should know what she wanted. When he didn't respond, she said in a mocking tone, "Sherry, darling."

"Of course. I don't suppose you could have poured yourself a glass instead of whacking me on the back of the head." He got up to serve her and she shook her head.

"Men can be so obtuse." She adjusted the sparkling, dangly earring that Amanda suspected might have been diamonds, knowing that José's family had been landowners for generations, perhaps since the Conquest. Why he chose to live with his wife at his in-laws rather than a place of their own, she did not know.

José came down the stairs and made his deliberate and elegant walk toward the group.

He drew the eyes of any woman in a room with his panther-like walk, dark hair and eyes contrasted with a pale complexion. There was a slight smile on his face, his usual expression, Amanda thought, as he approached and kissed his wife on the forehead.

"Don't muss my hair," she scolded without much conviction. The strawberry blonde bob with finger waves must have taken effort to perfect and she wasn't about to have her look ruined.

"Sherry?" Fred asked.

"Thank you," he answered in his only slightly accented baritone. "Good evening, Miss Burnside," he said, kissing Amanda's hand and then performing the same for Hextilda. He remained standing and held his cordial glass up in a toast to the company.

"How nice we're all here for dinner," Hextilda said.

"Oh, we're not staying," Caroline said. "We're going out to a club for dinner."

"Really, Caroline, you ought to have told me beforehand. Cook will be very cross."

Caroline gave her mother a withering look. "You can't be at the beck and call of your servants. They'll take terrible advantage of you," she drawled as she sipped her sherry.

Amanda was always surprised at how different the siblings were, not just in looks as Fred had brown hair and an angular face, but in attitudes and the way they spoke.

"That's fine. We've got Pavlova for dessert and now there'll be more for us," Hextilda said.

"What have you been doing these days?" Amanda asked José, whose employment situation was a mystery to her, if indeed he had to have a job, which she doubted.

"Business has been very slow lately. The imports get such scrutiny from the officials as if there was something illegal with handmade wooden furniture."

"I suppose they're on the lookout for alcohol," Fred said.

"Hidden in a finely carved mahogany table leg?" José laughed.

"No, but it could be in the packing materials. You never know."

José laughed again. "We make much more from our products that we would from a bottle of cheap gin." He drank the rest of his sherry in one gulp.

"I think people are on edge somehow," Amanda said. "Someone tried to break into our neighbor's home recently."

"What?" Hextilda was genuinely alarmed. "In this neighborhood?"

"Well, they wouldn't find anything to take from a North End home, would they?" Caroline said.

"It's a good thing Fred has a gun," Hextilda said.

Amanda didn't react outwardly, but her stomach clenched. "For hunting?" she asked.

"Those guns are up at the Castle," he said referring to their country home. "This is a handgun. I can't remember why I got it in the first place," he said looking somewhat puzzled. "Nor where it is."

"Ready to go, darling?" José asked his wife. She took one more sip of her sherry and said goodnight, her silk dress swishing as she passed by Amanda, leaving a trail of perfume.

"What have you been doing, Amanda? Fred tells me you are involved in renovations at the hospital." Before she had a chance to answer, a maid came in and announced that dinner was ready.

They walked slowly to the dining room as Amanda gave a brief description of the projects she was working on. They sat down and were served cream of cauliflower soup and talked about how medical care was difficult to attain for some people. The soup plates were removed, and the maid reentered.

"Excuse me, madame, but there is a telephone call for you."

Hextilda looked surprised.

"From New York. The man said that you had made an appointment to talk at this time."

"Oh, heavens. I think my brains are turning to mush. It's my editor and I've got to take this call. Please excuse me."

"Don't worry, Mother. We'll wait to eat."

"Better not. We are reviewing the latest manuscript and it may be a page-by-page dissection. I'll be at least an hour. You go ahead. I'll join you for dessert." She hurried out of the room.

"I don't understand it. She and that editor waste hours on the telephone when for the same cost, he could take a train up here and be done with it just as quickly. But, alone at last," he added, miming mustache twirling villains in the melodramas.

She smiled at his joke.

"Actually, I prefer not having the family around. Such drama. I've noticed when you're here, you're not as talkative as usual," he said.

The maid came back in with a plated meal for each of them rather than bringing out serving dishes since they were only two.

"It's a bit hard getting a word in with Caroline and your mother going on at each other," Amanda said.

"That's just their way. But they both adore you."

Amanda gave him a strange look. "No, I think they like me because you like me. I don't feel I have much in common with either of them except living in the same neighborhood." She was a bit surprised at how blunt that sounded, even if it were true.

Fred blinked and looked at his plate. "Mother was right. Cook has outdone herself." He took his knife and fork and sliced off a piece of veal Orloff. "She knows this is one of my favorites and bless her, it is fantastic as usual."

Amanda concurred. Their cook was just as technically accomplished, it was just that her mother didn't require such complicated dishes for an everyday meal. But perhaps this wasn't meant to be an everyday meal, she thought.

"You and Caroline have a lot in common, actually. The same upbringing and same kinds of schools. Her being two years older makes all the difference in who your friends are."

"True," Amanda admitted.

"And you're both independent in your attitudes. A bit rebellious in taking on work that women don't usually do. I admire that."

Amanda was beginning to wonder where the conversation was going until he put down his fork and knife and looked at her intently.

"I think we would make a good team, you and I. Oh, that's not how I meant to broach the subject—that sounds like we're playing football together. What I am trying to say is—."

"Fred, I am going to stop you there. I think I know what you're trying to say, and I need to tell you that I respect you tremendously but at this point in my life, I need to find out what I'm meant to do, and I can best do that by being single."

He sighed. "That independent and rebellious streak that I was just extolling has backfired on me." He paused, regrouping. "Don't you think that you could achieve what you are seeking even if you were married to me? I'd be supportive of what you'd like to do as long as it didn't mean trekking around the world solo."

Amanda smiled. "That isn't something I am keen to do, don't worry. What I want to do is to contribute to the community in some meaningful way, not just by heading a committee that raises money for the hospital."

"That's a worthy goal," Fred said.

"Yes, it is, but I've been distanced from the people it is meant to serve."

"Are you thinking of going into social work like Louisa?"

"I'm sorry to say that she is probably not interested in social work in any long-term way. Nor short term."

Fred cocked his head to the side in bewilderment. He resumed eating.

"I strongly suspect that she doesn't attend classes—I've never seen her studying or doing schoolwork—instead, I think it is a noble excuse for being out of sight of my parents all day. And I am beginning to understand how she spends her time."

"Don't keep me in suspense," Fred said, probably imagining the worst.

"She's had a secret boyfriend who stopped being a secret last summer when we were at the beach house in Maine. He's well mannered, knowledgeable about many things, handsome, it goes without saying, but he owns a club."

"An athletic club?" Fred asked.

"No," she laughed. "A nightclub. With a lively band, a sultry singer, a smoky atmosphere, dinner served and I'm guessing alcohol on the sly. Everything an upstanding family wants for their daughter."

"Now you've deftly managed to divert me from my formal proposal of marriage, and kudos to you for steering the conversation to another topic. But I am serious, Amanda. I think we could build a loving and meaningful life together. I'm not asking for an answer tonight, but I would appreciate it if you would give it serious thought. I offer my hand, my heart and a stable personality on which to build that."

Amanda nodded, indicating she would consider it. Fred might be stable and steady, but she thought his family was anything but that. And in any case, she was looking for that frisson that one should experience with a man you intended to marry, not what seemed like a business relationship.

Chapter 13

One thing she didn't share with Fred, and didn't intend to, was that she was due to come into an inheritance from her grandparents in February. She had known them only briefly as a child and they passed away when Louisa was still a baby. They had been generous in setting up a trust fund for each of them to be released at a certain age—not too young for them to squander it on frivolous items—but not too old that they could not make good use of it. The trust had been invested and grown significantly and the other stipulation, which was rare, was that the recipient had the choice of withdrawing it all at once or continuing with the current investment scheme and taking quarterly income. Amanda's parents were not pleased with this arrangement, fearing that some irrational decision would dissipate the funds too quickly and could have been one reason that they stressed frugality to their daughters. As it applied to people of their class, that is, so that Amanda had a car, which they judged was a practicality, but was dissuaded from taking noneducational, purely pleasure trips.

Ever since the beginning of the New Year, Louisa had been pestering her sister about the possibility of renting an apartment that they could share although it would be Amanda footing the bill until Louisa came into her money and able to contribute to the expenses. While the idea was appealing in many ways, there were so many more advantages to living with her parents and her independence hadn't been thwarted by staying at home.

Louisa was aware of Fred's interest in her sister and was ambivalent about the outcome. If Amanda were to get married, there went the idea of sharing an apartment. She would be able to rent something on her own by then, but it would have to be something significantly smaller. If Amanda left, Louisa would be under more intense scrutiny by her parents about her activities and she couldn't keep up the ruse of being invested in social work as a volunteer and certainly not as a profession, which was not in her interest at all. If Amanda rejected Fred's proposal, she would stay at home, continue to provide transportation to Louisa, act as a cover in some cases, and dilute their parents' interest in her comings and goings. What was best for Amanda was not among the factors involved in Louisa's calculation of what was best for herself.

The crease between Amanda's eyes when she returned from dinner at the Brownes told Louisa, who was getting over a cold and stayed at home that night, that all was not settled between the two. Being ever so sympathetic, she asked her sister if she would like a cup of tea in the kitchen since the staff had gone home for the night.

"I didn't know you knew how to boil water," Amanda said to her sister who was in pajamas and a dressing gown fiddling with lighting the gas range.

"Very funny. You forget that Mother had me take a class in menu preparation with Miss What's-her-name. Very boring. What vegetables go with what meat, keeping a record of what you served and who was present so you wouldn't have the horror of serving the same dish to someone on a subsequent visit. You'd think they were marrying us off to one of the princes of Europe or something."

"If they did, you would have someone on your staff to keep track of all that. And if you didn't, you didn't need those lessons. I went through it, too, and I agree, it seemed ridiculous. But you never know. The Prince of Wales is still single. You'll just have to get yourself over to London and insert yourself into one of his parties. He's in the newsreels all the time. England's 'Most Eligible Bachelor.'"

"Royal life might not be all that much fun," Louisa said, tilting her head as she lit the burner to make sure the fire caught the gas under the kettle. "Do you suppose Queen Mary ever wanders around Buckingham Palace in her pajamas and dressing gown?"

They both laughed at the image of the woman they had seen in photos and newsreels in full regalia and jewels, stiff backed and dour, lounging about in her nightclothes.

Turning from the stove, Louisa gave her sister a piercing look. "So, Fred proposed?"

"What makes you think that?"

"By your distracted manner and the sound of the wheels turning in your brain as you weigh the advantages and disadvantages of such a union."

"Well…."

"Aha! I knew it. He's a steady, stable sort of fellow. Well regarded in the community. Good looking but a bit dull in a social sense."

Amanda reared her head back in defense. "That's not a kind evaluation of who he is."

"I think it is. And what's wrong with that? He's never going to run off with a young nurse or put a foot wrong with you. He obviously loves you. What's the matter with that?"

Amanda took a deep breath and retrieved a teapot from the pantry and a tin of tea leaves to buy herself some time before answering.

"There's nothing the matter with him. It's his family that is off-putting. His mother is very strange, theatrical, dramatic and she writes those awful, cheap books."

"I bet she makes a mint from those books."

"You may be right. There's his sister who is beautiful and condescending—nothing like Fred in her attitude and interests. Seemingly indulged since infancy and now married to a wealthy and gorgeous husband. But then, there was an older brother, who no one talks about. We don't have any skeletons in the closet, do we?"

"If we do, I haven't found the right closet." She sat down opposite her sister at the big table that served as a preparation area for the family and a gathering place for the servants during the day.

"I haven't given him an answer. I do like him tremendously, but I haven't been stricken with Cupid's arrow, if you know what I mean."

"As long as we're laying our souls out bare in this humble setting, let me say that I have experienced the 'colpo di fulmine' as the Italians say," Louisa said.

"Since when do you know Italian?"

Louisa deflected the question by busying herself getting the teacups and saucers on the table, then cream and sugar.

"One hears it from time to time."

"All right, my love life aside, I want to know what's going on with you and Rob Worley. I know you're at his club more than anywhere else and that your interest in social work was manufactured to seem like a true avocation, but in reality, it gives you time to be out of the house most of the day. How you have managed to be at his club at night is another matter."

Louisa smiled. "Your car keys left on the hook by the back door for transportation and the back stairs for my return."

Amanda was annoyed that she had been so dense as not to realize the extent to which her sister had pulled the wool over their eyes.

"Now, you recall when we were at the beach house last summer Rob came up and Mother and Daddy were prepared to be horrified and assumed he was some sort of gangster with a toothpick dangling from his mouth. Obviously, he did not meet that expectation and showed himself to be a polite, erudite and, might I add, quite handsome man, who has been successful in these difficult financial times. He won them over during that entire incident and they should be happy that I am involved with someone who has my best interests at heart." The kettle whistled and Louisa very carefully poured the boiling water into the teapot and put a cozy on top to keep it warm while it brewed.

"Does he?" Amanda asked. "I don't doubt his affection for you, but he might still be a gangster of some sort."

"Don't use that word so loosely," Louisa said. "Owning a club doesn't make one a 'gangster.' He's making an honest living, even if it doesn't measure up to your definition of what is respectable."

"All right then. I'd like to visit his club and see what's what."

"All right," Louisa said. "Why don't you come over tomorrow evening. And bring Fred."

"I'll come tomorrow. But I'll bring Detective Halloran instead, just to make sure everything is on the up and up."

Chapter 14

Amanda had called Detective Halloran in the afternoon almost wishing that he would not pick up the phone. She imagined this must be what it was like for a man to ask a woman out on a date—although this was nothing like a date. Still, she considered it forward behavior before convincing herself that she was acting in the best interests of her sister and family. However, he answered after the first ring and seemed pleased by the request.

"Of course, I'd be glad to accompany you. I've been curious as to what goes on in that place and didn't want to go in by myself and cause a stir. Being on the police force and all."

"Yes, but in a sense that's why I wanted you especially," and at that word she cringed before going on, "because you are attuned to what is legitimate and what is not."

"One thing I am not going to do is arrest anyone for drinking alcohol. But neither am I going to consume any on the premises. Just to keep things straight with the owner."

"I understand completely."

"Shall I pick you up at your house?"

"No," she answered quickly and thought how to amend her response. "I wouldn't want my parents to think that I was getting further involved in the business of Mr. Harris' death or investigation." She thought that sounded weak but blundered on. "I'll meet you at the station and we can go to the club in my car if it is more inconspicuous."

"That won't be necessary. It will look strange that you are driving me somewhere. I do have my own car and it's not marked Police in big white letters on the side."

That got a laugh from her, and they settled on eight o'clock, late for the older generation of Burnsides to be going out but early for the club crowd. After she hung up, she had to give some thought to what she should wear. An evening gown would look ridiculously formal, and she couldn't wear her day clothes. She went to Louisa's room and found her putting her hair into elaborate waves secured with bobby pins.

"Getting ready so soon?" Amanda asked.

"Just trying something out I saw in a magazine. It's more complicated than I imagined."

Amanda sat on the bed watching her sister seated at her vanity with a three-paneled mirror that allowed her to turn her head from one side to the other to see herself from all angles.

"What do you think?"

"It looks complicated, if that's what you were hoping to achieve." Amanda wore her hair in a simple bob and couldn't be bothered with anything more ornate. She glanced toward Louisa's closet. "Say, what do you wear when you go out to the club?"

Her sister turned to face her and gave a giggle. "What do you imagine?"

"I don't know. That's why I'm asking you. I don't think I have anything suitable."

"Are you thinking of going?" When her sister didn't answer, she continued, "You want something that is modern. Stylish. Chic."

"Show me," Amanda said.

Louisa pulled the hangers across the support rod one by one until she came to a dress that she took out and held against her. "Like this one." It was floor length, deep blue, with a defined waist, V-neck and short split sleeves that fluttered when she moved it from side to side. "I can add a belt or a pin to change the look."

"Wherever did you get that?"

Without answering, Louisa took out a dress in mauve with boat neckline and full, short sleeves.

"I'll try that one," Amanda said, making sure the door was locked from any intrusion by her mother before taking off her day clothes.

"Here, I'll zip you up," Louisa said.

"It's a bit scratchy in the shoulders," Amanda complained.

"Just some crinoline to fluff out the sleeves. It fits you well."

Amanda looked at herself in the tall mirror in front of the windows. "It does accentuate my waist and is only a little too short in length." She turned around and noticed the low cut of the back.

"You can wear a short jacket if you're uncomfortable."

"I'd better have something to wear, or I'll freeze to death."

"I guess that means you'll be borrowing it?"

"Yes, thank you for the offer."

Louisa dug through a drawer in her dresser and produced a corsage of white silk flowers and held it up to her sister's right shoulder.

"I know you've got the other accessories, but if you need help, we'll fuss around after dinner tonight. When are you going out?"

"Eight."

"Better use the back stairs."

$\sim$

AMANDA HAD BEEN to her share of dances, parties and balls but the notion of going to a nightclub was something new and she didn't know what to expect. When she approached the police station, what she didn't imagine was Detective Halloran standing out front dressed in evening clothes under an overcoat, and she could see at least one of his colleagues peer through the glass-topped doors to see who had pulled up. Halloran got in and tipped his hat and suggested they drive around back to park and then take his car.

As he opened the passenger side door for her, he commented, "If you don't mind, I'd prefer in this circumstance for you to call me Brendan and I'll call you Amanda. Whatever you say, please don't refer to me as detective."

"Naturally. Although it makes it seem as though we are on some undercover assignment."

Starting the engine, he turned to her and said, "This is anything but that."

That comment got her back up as she thought he meant she was pretending to play cops and robbers. Then it occurred to her that he considered this a date and that she had asked him out. The thought made her go silent as they drove through the city to the neighborhood well-known for clubs and entertainment and she scoured the streets for some sign of illegal activity. All she saw were people dressed up as Louisa had described, walking quickly because of the cold from one establishment to another.

"It's called club-hopping, and you'll see a lot of that here. Folks sit for a while listening to music in one place, have a drink—or not—and then decide to go to another club to see who's there. And the place that's most crowded is where you want to be seen."

"Why?"

He looked at her as if she could not be serious. "To be seen, of course. It's why some club owners go out of their way to cater to people others might recognize or have seen in photos in the newspapers."

"I suppose that makes sense if that's one's purpose in life. To be seen." Even as she said it, Amanda realized it sounded dismissive, especially since anyone who saw her enter Worley's club, called the Oasis, would assume that was why she was there.

They pulled up in front and a doorman in a garish outfit with a turban opened the passenger side for Amanda while a valet trotted to the driver's side to retrieve the keys from Brendan. They looked up at the neon sign with an image of a palm tree arched over the name and then at each other, realizing they were in for some Arabian Nights-themed place.

Upon entry, it was more subdued than the doorman's outfit would suggest, with murals of sand dunes adorning the walls, a starry night depicted on the ceiling and potted palms that in a more upscale part of town could be a tearoom called Palm Court. The plants were placed to give the illusion of privacy between tables, but the fronds were up so high that everyone in the place was visible once visitors made it past the cloakroom. The exception was what looked to be private rooms screened from the main area by Moorish latticework that hid prying eyes from seeing who was within. The place was packed and a band on a platform at the far end was accompanying the sultry voice of a singer dressed in a clingy black dress that offset her auburn hair.

"I hope we can get a table," Amanda said as they stood at the top of a short staircase surveying the scene.

Brendan raised his chin and a maître d' appeared, practically bowing and scraping.

"Yes, Monsieur?" he asked, leaning forward to hear.

"Table for two, please."

"Right this way," he said, snaking between the tables and the people making their way back from the dance floor.

"Do you come here often?" Amanda said, jokingly.

"Every now and then," he answered, and she didn't know if he was serious or not.

They were interrupted by Rob Worley, who appeared out of nowhere, dapper in a white jacket that showed off his tanned face.

"Please, Henri, I'll take care of it," and he ushered them toward the front of the room to a small table just opposite a larger one where Louisa sat, casually smoking a cigarette. Worley joined her, whispering something in her ear.

"Hello," Amanda said as nonchalantly as she could manage to her sister, surprised that she smoked and noted how at ease she seemed in the noisy atmosphere where she was the center of attention. They sat and Amanda smiled at their own tiny table, barely large enough to hold two dinner plates, but it was ingenious on Worley's part since he could get more people in the place and whatever sized plates came their way would look huge by comparison. It also afforded two people to be seated very close together, another plus considering the sound of the band, the singer and the people chattering throughout.

Henri reappeared almost immediately and asked what they would like to have.

"Two champagne cocktails, please," Brendan said.

"I'm afraid we don't serve alcohol, sir. But I could get you some sparkling water." He awaited a nod and left quickly.

"Do you think everyone in this place knows what I do for a living?" Brendan asked, noticing that several women were looking at him.

Amanda was surprised that he had no idea how dashing he looked with his almost black hair and blue eyes that would draw women's eyes to him. But it was not just his appearance, it was the way he moved confidently, coupled with a hint of danger, that caught people's attention.

The singer had finished her song, nodded to the applause, and left the stage while the band played something softly to mask the chatter of the crowd.

"Now that we're here, I'm wondering why I made you come with me," Amanda said.

"I think you were thinking you could catch two birds with one stone. Find out what your sister was up to and slumming with an Irishman." He said it with a smile, but there was an edge to his words.

"Do you suppose you're the first Irishman I've ever encountered?"

"I mean besides the gardener and man who hauls your trash."

"Don't make assumptions about me, sir. You have no idea who I know and what I do most of the day." She looked away, stung by his casual rudeness. She saw Caroline and her husband José making their way through the room up to Worley's table and they greeted one another warmly. It was then that Caroline caught sight of Amanda and swept a gaze over the man by her side, and it seemed as if she couldn't wait to come over and discover what was going on.

"Good evening," she said to Amanda before raising her eyes at the sight of Brendan. He stood up and said good evening but did not give his name. Nor did Amanda make an introduction, not sure whether she ought to or if Caroline would be offended that she wasn't here with her brother Fred. Not that Fred would frequent such a place.

"You don't have a name?" Caroline asked him.

"Sadly, no. They left that off my birth certificate."

Caroline laughed. "Come on, then, No Name why don't you join us?"

"Is there enough room?" Amanda asked seeing that Worley's table was bigger than theirs but hardly large enough for six to sit comfortably.

"We'll get another table to move next to it." She went back to her husband and said something to him, he looked back toward the entrance and a waiter swiftly came to see what was needed.

"They're very accommodating here," Amanda said, surprised at the resolution of the space issue in a matter of minutes as another tiny table was brought adjacent to the larger one.

Henri arrived with the drinks, served in coupe glasses. He bowed and left, and they each took a sip.

"Oh, dear, it is really champagne," Amanda said softly.

"Of course. He wants to make sure to compromise me if it comes to that." He got up and escorted her to the table where Caroline was gesturing them to sit. Introductions were made and Brendan gave his real name, which didn't shock anyone as Amanda had supposed.

"José is one of the silent partners," Caroline said in a low tone.

"Not so silent now, my dear," José added.

"How did you get interested in the restaurant business?" Brendan asked.

"One must do something and much of our business back home was disrupted by the new person in office."

"Confiscated, is what he means," Louisa clarified.

Amanda was fascinated by her sister's transformation from the awkward debutante who was nervous about having her formal portrait taken to the sophisticated young woman at the center of this club atmosphere.

After a round of conversation, Brendan pulled Worley aside, had a brief word and they left toward the back of the room. After being tricked by the champagne, he thought he would inflict a little embarrassment on his host by asking to view the basement. Worley well knew who he was dealing with and didn't bat an eye when he took them through a long hallway and a door at the end that led to the basement. A beefy man came out from behind one of the doors they passed and walked quietly behind Halloran.

"We're in tight quarters here, so we need to find any available space to store things." The area was well lit and clean with boxes stacked one upon another. "Aldo, why don't you show the gentleman what we keep down here."

The other man obliged, taking a knife from his pocket and snicking it open, sliced through the topmost box. Inside were bags of sugar, tea and coffee. He was about to open the next box when Halloran held up his hand.

"Looks good to me. How did you meet José?" he asked casually.

"I really can't remember. Possibly through Louisa and then Caroline. He was itching for something to do once the political winds changed back home. These Latin American banana republics turn over rapidly and folks need to get their money out and working in some other business until it's time to return to power." He smiled and Halloran nodded.

"The wheel of fortune turning endlessly," he said.

"And his wife has a lot of money," Worley added, which Halloran suspected not to be true. "Let's go back upstairs. I wouldn't want Amanda to think we shanghaied you."

"That was the last thing on my mind," he said but wondered if that very thing had happened to Amanda after he came back upstairs to find her absent from the table.

"She went to powder her nose," Caroline said. "Oh, look, Sofia is coming out to do another number."

The lights dimmed slightly, and the songstress walked out in a different dress with a high neck and a low back and waited for the intro from the band before launching into her song.

Amanda really was powdering her nose, seated at a vanity when Louisa sat beside her.

"You could have knocked me over with a feather bringing him here," she said.

"You didn't bat an eyelash," Amanda said.

"It's just practice. I'm surprised Caroline didn't react more," Louisa said.

"She did. But she was more interested in flirting with him."

"Why did you bring Halloran?"

"Who better to check up on you and this establishment?"

"All you had to do was ask me."

"All right then. Is everything on the up and up?" Amanda asked.

Louisa paused while applying her lipstick. "That's a complicated question."

"You know it's not if they're serving alcohol."

"Don't be a hypocrite. We serve it at home."

"I have a feeling Daddy's stash pre-dates the Volstead Act."

"Anyway, they only serve it to special guests. And Rob made sure the detective got some as a little joke. He knows the police would never make a raid here." Louisa swiveled in the chair to face her sister. "But if you would like to see a real speakeasy, we can go down the street. Your date might not want to be seen there, but I can tell you the Police Chief is a frequent guest." She got up.

"But we just got here," Amanda said, surprised at the suggestion.

"It's called club hopping, dear. Let's go."

Chapter 15

Amanda could tell that Brendan wasn't entirely convinced that going to a speakeasy was a good idea but the entire group at the table was enthusiastic to visit the one nearby that promised lively music and surprising guests.

Brendan helped Amanda into her coat, and they followed the other two couples out into the cold with Rob waving off the valet indicating that they were going to walk, not drive. The wind was icy and so were some of the sidewalks, but the women clung to their partners and no mishaps occurred as they walked two blocks and then into an alley marked 'Dead End.' It had the requisite trash cans and cat that scrambled over a wall as they picked their way over the cobblestones and saw that they were coming up to a brick wall. Rob veered left and disappeared from view; the others followed, finding out that there was an opening masked by another partial wall. To the right was a green door and he knocked on it. A small wooden aperture in the door slid open and the pair of eyes on the other side blinked and the aperture was rapidly closed. Then the green door opened, and they found themselves in a vestibule lined with a few chairs and another door about ten feet away.

Without speaking, Rob opened it and they descended. The first indication that it wasn't just some strange basement they were entering was a slight throb felt in the cement stairs and a whiff of cigarette smoke. At the bottom of the stairs was another door that took them down a long hall where the pulsations were more pronounced until they reached a final door that opened up to a scene of loud music, talking and abundant cigarette smoke.

They checked their outer garments at the cloakroom while becoming accustomed to the haze of smoke and the noise which made conversation more of a shouting match. Louisa nodded her head in one direction, and they were taken to a small room off the main floor where they could talk and be heard, observe but not necessarily be seen.

"What did I tell you? The Police Chief is here. Now might be your opportunity to say hello, Brendan," Louisa said.

"I think I'll wait a bit."

The Chief was in lively conversation with Ron King, each with an arm around a young woman, not likely their wives. Their exact words could not be overheard but it seemed a friendly interaction as they sipped their drinks.

Almost immediately a waiter appeared, and Rob ordered drinks, Amanda wondering if the alcohol would be safe and then jettisoning her worry as she saw no one else seemed concerned.

"Rob's got his own here, so we know it's the good stuff." Louisa said. Her sister noticed that her language was more colloquial in that atmosphere; her parents would be horrified.

A bottle appeared on the table along with a bowl of ice, a pitcher of water, and glasses. Rob did the honors and poured two fingers for each of them saying, "Straight in from Canada." He nodded toward Brendan and added, "From what I hear." He shrugged his shoulders as if he was not a party to smuggling and it was of no concern to him where the alcohol had come from.

They sipped what was top of the line aged whiskey that nobody would dare to vilify with anything other than water and by the looks on the faces around the table, everyone thought it was superb.

"I heard that most of the stuff comes into Detroit from Canada, is that true?" José asked.

Rob hid a smile and seemed to continue the game. "I wouldn't know. It's what someone who gave it to me said."

"As a non-native, I was just curious," José said, and his wife shot him a look.

"I'm glad that Boston is not the point of entry," Brendan said. "Being such a large port and all." He smiled and that got a laugh from the men.

There was a drum roll, and someone stepped up to the microphone and announced the name of the band, which was lost in the noise of conversation. Nonetheless, the music began, and it was nothing like what they had heard at the Oasis. This was raw and so loud that it could be felt pulsing through the air. Some people got up to dance but the politicians and bureaucrats present demurred and moved toward the sides of the room to continue their discussions. At one point, Brendan did a double take at the entrance of another man, the Mayor. He backslapped both the Police Chief and King and waved his hand in the air indicating he needed a drink.

Amanda knew the Mayor by sight, having seen his face plastered in the newspapers as often as he could manage, but she leaned over to Brendan to ask who the other two men were. He told her and her eyebrows raised.

"Perhaps I should say good evening to them," he said. Turning to Rob he asked where the facilities were and left their private space to go out into the throng, some dancing, many sitting, talking and laughing loudly, over toward the spot where the three men stood. Ron King recognized him and shook his hand and introduced him to the Mayor. The Police Chief looked astounded to encounter the detective in that place but amended his reaction shortly thereafter and pounded him on the back as if he weren't such a stuck-up fellow after all. A few more words, Brendan made his way to the men's room wondering what the conversation would be about after he left. He hoped his presence there should have dispelled what negative impression the Chief had had of him previously.

Amanda sensed an undercurrent in the conversation that was taking place between Rob and José that she couldn't put a finger on. They clearly knew one another very well and were in business together, but what that entailed was not entirely clear. Obviously, there was the Oasis, but were they smuggling alcohol into the States from Canada? Was this speakeasy his, too? Was the joke on her? She sipped her drink until Brendan came back.

"Would you like something to eat?" he asked her.

She wasn't particularly hungry, and Louisa gave her head a small shake. "They don't specialize in food at this place," she said.

"Who were you talking to?" Amanda asked.

"Ron King, the former Deputy Director in the Buildings Department and since the demise of Mr. Harris, the new Director. That's why he is snuggling up to the Mayor."

"Ah," Amanda said. "They still haven't released the permit for the clinic. Do you think I should ask him why?"

Brendan looked at her and smiled. "I don't see why not. Let me introduce you."

They got up and he took her to the threesome and told them that she was part of the group who were renovating the clinic for Mercy Hospital.

"The Indigent Children's Clinic?" the Mayor asked.

"Yes."

"Wonderful work you all do there," he said.

"I'm not a nurse. I've been working with the Director, Mr. Barlow, on the designs for the renovation. We'd do better work if we got our permit processed," she said, smiling at Mr. King.

He began to stammer about the mess he had to clean up with the former director and the shortage of staff and was muttering about something else when the Mayor interrupted him.

"Come on, man! Let's get that moving. My constituents rely on that clinic—it's a life saver for many families."

"How good of you to say so," Amanda said. "We were just talking this week of putting additional clinics into the neighborhoods, on a smaller scale, of course, so people won't have to travel so far to access services."

"What a good idea. Come to my office sometime soon and we can talk about places that might be vacant, like the Hibernian Hall in the daytime or some churches. I like this girl!" he declared, his round red cheeks glowing with the idea he had just generated.

"Thank you," Amanda smiled, and they made their way back toward the private room.

"Do you think your work here is done?" she asked Brendan.

"Yes, I've seen all that Rob was willing to show me. Which was nothing."

"Would you prefer to get out of here before there is a raid?"

He stopped to look at her in concern. "With the Mayor and Police Chief here? Are you serious? No, but I've had enough noise, cigarette smoke and dubious company—your sister excluded, of course."

"I'm not so sure," Amanda said.

They made their excuse to the group that they were expected at work the next day, not an issue for the others, and made their way through the crowd and the labyrinthine exit, the noise receding to silence by the time they reached the green door. The doorman nodded to them and let them out into the cold alley, where even a hobo looking for a quiet spot to sleep for the night would not suspect what went on down below.

"Would you like to go back to the Oasis?" Brendan asked.

"Thank you, but I think I've had enough clubbing for the evening. I suppose if a person doesn't need to get up in the morning for a job, staying out to all hours is fine."

"That may be true of Rob and José, but many others there will have to report to an office with a throbbing head tomorrow. And it's not even midnight," he said, looking briefly at his watch as they passed under a streetlight.

He retrieved his car and drove Amanda to hers that was parked in the lot next to the station, probably the safest place for it to be at this hour besides the garage at home. He got in the passenger side of her car and waited for her to start it and agreed to stay until the engine was warm enough to drive back.

"Unless you would like me to follow you home, just in case."

"Yes, that would be nice. Preferable to you walking back from Beacon Hill, Detective Halloran."

"Ah, so we are we back to the formalities, Miss Burnside?"

"It's probably for the best. Your boss and the Mayor wouldn't mind, but my parents would not approve."

"Well, then. Goodnight, Miss Burnside. It has been an informative and enjoyable evening. Perhaps we can do it again sometime."

"Thank you, I'll look into my engagement book for an opening."

With a smile he got out and proceeded to his car and waited for her to take hers out into the street before following. All areas of the city were familiar to him, even Beacon

Hill, where she was headed, the enclave of the old Yankee families where people of his acquaintance were working as servants. They considered themselves lucky as many places still had 'Irish Need Not Apply' signs when looking for work. The old guard was cutting off its own nose to save its face, he thought, as the Irish Americans were becoming more prosperous and might displace the older generation soon. And behind them had already come other waves of immigrants taking nothing for granted and willing to do whatever work had to be done to survive. The wheel of fortune constantly turning.

Chapter 16

Halloran was glad he had been careful not to drink very much the night before but felt fuzzy headed all the same in the morning. He lived alone in one side of the duplex his father owned; the other side rented out. It made sense for him to leave the family home in Dorchester because his late hours were a visible worry to his mother, who felt he needed to have a hot meal whatever time he came home. Then one of his sisters returned home with her newly unemployed husband and their baby. The house had been crowded enough with his siblings and the addition of three people, the smallest of whom had to be catered to day and night by being passed from one aunt or uncle to another. Then there was the bickering between his sister and her husband who she didn't think was being serious enough in looking for work once they had become housed. Halloran's father, who had done manual labor most of his life before, had been silent but disapproving, and his mother played her usual role of peacemaker. To relieve the pressure of so many people and strained relationships, Brendan Halloran decided to move out, to the shock of his parents.

"I'll be closer to work, there'll be less fuss about my hours, and Ma, you won't have to keep my supper warm because I'm working late."

"What will you eat?" she had asked, incredulous that a grown man could feed himself.

"He'll tear off pieces of the wallpaper. Add some salt and pepper!" his younger brother had said, getting a light punch on the arm in return.

"You'd better not touch that wallpaper!" their mother said, having great pride in their ability to own a rental unit.

He paid them rent, oversaw the tenant next door and within one more year he would have enough for a down payment for a duplex of his own. As he went to work, he scanned the houses on either side of the street to see if there were any 'For Sale' signs or indications that homes had been vacated. Since times were hard, some families owing back rent took the opportunity to leave in the dead of night.

He was barely in the front doors of the station when he could hear a dog barking and the sergeant on duty hailed him.

"Mother of God! The racket! You've got to help us here. We've got two men out with the flu and this hobo shows up last night after picking a fight with one of our own, then tells a wild story of people chasing after him. And he brings in his dog, to boot!"

"Let me get some coffee and I'll go down to the tank to see what's what," Halloran said.

The coffee was not very good, but he couldn't make much better in his place, so he took a cup, sipped it, and took his time ignoring the noise from below where they kept their 'guests' as they liked to call them.

The man in question was calmly seated on a bench in a cell, his dog by his side now quiet, but any disturbance, such as someone new coming into view, set him off barking again. At Halloran's entrance to the cells, the man stood up. He wore what must have been a larger man's cast-off that came down to his ankles with a rope belt and the filthy cuffs rolled back exposing bony wrists.

"There you are. I've been waiting to tell my story to someone but those coppers in their stuffy uniforms didn't want to hear what I had to say."

"All right, I'm all ears."

"Sit," the man said to the dog who obeyed. He was a sturdy Boston Terrier whose tongue lolled out of his mouth. "He needs to go out. You know."

"I don't doubt it. But tell me your story first." Halloran allowed the man to sit back down while he stood outside the cell.

"First, this is not my dog. But I didn't steal him."

"Okay." Looking down on the intake form, Halloran said, "It says your name is Crouse."

"Edwin Crouse. That's me."

"And you were taken in for assaulting a policeman? That wasn't very wise."

"I know, but he wouldn't listen. Times are hard and I can't find enough food for myself, much less for this one. I can't just let him loose again, so I thought I'd tell where I found him. There's got to be an owner. Look at the nice collar and leash."

What Halloran noticed was a ratty cloth tied around the dog's midsection. "Was he wearing that?"

"Nah, I put that on him to keep him warm although he keeps me warm at night. So, as I was trying to tell the cop earlier, I was walking through Boston Common one night, looking for a place to bed down. I hear an argument, then a shot and this dog starts barking. I call him Barney although I bet that's not his real name. Anyhow, the dog starts to charge at the man—."

"What man?"

"The man that is still standing in the walkway. And then the guy disappears into the bushes and the dog starts running toward me. I don't know what to do. I like dogs, but this one don't know me. But he's scared and I have to chase him a bit to grab his leash. I wanted to see what the shot was all about, but my good sense tells me the guy has a gun. And I don't want to get hit, so when I see some other people coming down the walkway, I took off."

"What other people?"

"It was a couple. That's all I could see. It was dark."

"Are you sure it was a man you saw standing there before?"

A nod.

"Only one?"

"That's all I saw. Now, can I take him out for a leak? Me, too, if you don't mind."

"The gents' is up the hall. I'll wait with Barney here and you and I will take him outside for his constitutional. Then back inside and I want a more detailed description of what you saw."

Crouse nodded and Halloran got someone to let him out while he held the leash of the dog who didn't bother to see who held it. This was undoubtedly Patrick Harris' dog that had witnessed the whole episode of his owner's murder yet could provide no clues of any use. After a long discussion with Crouse, Halloran gained no more useful information but at least could return the animal to the owner's wife. He asked Crouse if he had an address; of course not, otherwise why would he be looking for a place to sleep in a park in January? But he told him he could stay for the rest of the day as two meals would be provided. Then they would drop the charges.

"Gee, thanks."

Halloran called the widow first, then put Barney in the back seat of a patrol car and drove him to Brookline. Mrs. Harris was waiting behind the front door and when they pulled up, she ran out with a coat over her apron.

"Pepper!" she called out and the car door was barely open before he ran out to meet her as she stooped down and put her arms around his shoulders. She cried and he whimpered and Halloran walked up to them.

"I'm sorry for your loss. Someone brought your dog into the station."

"Why did he do that to Patrick?"

"I'm afraid we're no closer to finding out who killed your husband, but I don't think it was the hobo who caught your dog on Boston Common. He just happened to be there after the fact."

"Come inside, please," she said, wiping the tears from her face. Then to the dog, "Look at how dirty you are! And where did that dreadful coat come from?" She kept up scolding the dog as he waddled up the stairs to the front door all the way into the foyer.

"I've met you before," Mrs. Harris said. She took off the scarf that had been wrapped around her head and Halloran was surprised to see that she was younger than he remembered.

She invited him in to have coffee, walking through the large living room and asking him to wait there while she fetched it. He could hear her rattling around in the kitchen two rooms away and he looked around at the well-furnished room that spoke of her late husband's stature in the city bureaucracy. That is, until he died, and his reputation was ruined. Halloran knew that there was some funeral payout to the family of a serving official, but it was one time only and scarcely could continue to support the widow. Would she be able to keep the house?

She came back into the living room with a small tray and two cups of coffee and a plate of cookies. He thanked her and she sat down, expecting more information than he knew he could provide.

"We haven't had much luck, I'm afraid to say. Just a mention that another man was present, but no detailed description to help."

"I don't understand it. Patrick was well liked and no matter what anyone says, I know he did a good job. He was always well-organized here at home. How could he be negligent at work? It doesn't make any sense."

"No, it doesn't."

"And why was he walking Pepper all the way on Boston Common?"

"Did someone contact him that night?"

"The phone rang late in the afternoon, but he answered it and said it was someone trying to sell something."

"He didn't seem concerned or worried?"

"Not at all. He went down to the basement and tinkered around on the workbench fixing something. It wasn't until later that he said he'd walk Pepper. I had no idea he had taken the car until he didn't come back." The tears were starting. "This is the worst thing that has ever happened to me," she said softly.

"I'm sorry," Halloran repeated.

She fiddled with a button on the front of her skirt. "I'll have to go back to my parents in New Hampshire. I can't afford to stay here by myself. The neighbors would be up in arms if I were to take in boarders and I'd be the object of a lot of gossip." She chewed her lip.

Halloran swallowed the last of the coffee and thanked her again. "We'll be sure to let you know if we find out anything." She nodded and he put his coat back on and let himself out. A deep breath of cold air tempered his feelings, and he went back to the car trying to make sense of a murder that seemingly made no sense.

Chapter 17

That same day, Amanda was at the hospital meeting with Mr. Barlow when Miss Bailey knocked on the door and told him that a Mr. King was there to see him. He got to his feet, remarking, "Maybe this is our permit at last," and left to greet the man who was all smiles.

Barlow invited him into his office and King was surprised to see Amanda there, snapped his fingers and pointed at her.

"You sure knew how to make things move," he said by way of a compliment, but the look he gave her was not positive. He unfurled the permit as if it were some precious document, which in fact it was, but he was overly theatrical in his presentation.

"That's wonderful. We can get the crew working."

"I saw some men out there already. They haven't been working without a permit, have they?" King asked.

"I think the contractor allowed them to be in the building in expectation of getting this. He didn't want to let them go and not be able to assemble another crew."

"Are you kidding? In times like these, your grandmother would be happy to have a job." His laugh was a little too loud. "If there is anything else the City of Boston can do for you, just let me know," he added, getting up and shaking hands with Barlow. He nodded at Amanda with a tight smile on his florid face.

They waited until he was in the elevator and on his way down before examining the permit and making sure it was the document they needed.

"About time," Barlow muttered. "Did you have something to do with this?"

"Of course not. I don't know what he was talking about. Would you like me to take this down to the clinic building?"

"I think it's supposed to be posted in a certain way. We should have asked when he was still here. Obviously, we can't post it outside, perhaps just inside the front door if someone wants to check."

Amanda took it from him and went to get her coat before taking the elevator down to the first floor. As she walked out the back door toward the clinic, she could see Ron King was on the site and hurried to ask him about the protocol for putting up the permit. But he wasn't just looking around, he was in a shouting match with the foreman and Amanda wondered if this was what the building trades were all about: arguing and shouting. They fell silent when she approached, and King was all smarmy smiles again.

She felt the wariness of the other workers, two of whom were standing in front of the corrugated metal shed, arms crossed, taking in the scene. The others were frozen in place, some holding tools as if they were about to launch an attack before beginning to move around.

The tension dissipated, King asked if she needed anything.

"We've got the permit, thank you very much, now what are we supposed to do with it? Hang it on a nail inside?" she asked sharply.

"That's one thing to do with it," he answered and rather than engaging in a further sarcastic exchange, Amanda went inside the cold building and found an available thumb tack in the bulletin board hanging in the makeshift office. She jammed the pin into the board saying to herself, "Now, we're finally in business."

By the time she had exited the building, Ron King was gone, and the foreman was now giving orders to the workmen in his usual loud voice, and she wondered if that was the only type of communication of which he was capable.

Once inside the hospital, she tracked down Fred and asked what his schedule was for the day. Since he had started early, he intended to leave about five o'clock.

"My father drove me here today as my car needed servicing. I was wondering if you could give me a lift home?"

"And dinner?"

"If you like," she said, trying not to sound unenthusiastic but hoping that he wasn't going to bring up the marriage issue again. She would just have to maneuver the conversation into other topics.

Mr. Barlow was in high spirits and was on the phone with the contractor giving him the good news while beckoning Amanda into his office. He hung up the instrument and beamed a smile. "Full steam ahead! I think you can start to get some estimates on the work you had proposed. The Board has allocated a budget, and you want to be sure that what you intend falls into that amount."

Amanda smiled, although she felt a chill in her stomach realizing she may have oversold herself on the project. Planning was one thing but now she was expected to follow through to the end of the project. She had never asked anyone for a bid on anything. In her personal life, she paid what people told her the price of something was. Now she had to take the lead and be more precise about what she wanted, but still didn't know if there was a formal process. Better ask.

"Do I have to draw up a written document first for each business whose goods or services we'll need?"

Mr. Barlow caught on immediately. "It is typical to put together your requirements, what they call the 'specs' and then get three bids from three different suppliers and compare them. You'll be looking to compare not just price but the reputation of the company, if they deliver on time, the quality of the goods, and obviously the price. Feel free to ask around to get endorsements or lack thereof as you weigh the results. It will take some time to put the specifications together and you'll need to give the businesses time to price things out. I imagine it will be some weeks since the work on the building is just getting started."

"Thank you," Amanda said.

"Let me know if you need any help or want me to look over any part of the process."

She left his office wondering: *Ask around? Ask who?* It wasn't as if she had ever ordered four dozen reception room chairs before in her life. Despite reservations about her ability to go from the creative development to the more practical portion of the project, she sat down in the small office down the hall and started writing down what she needed. Amanda soon realized that the elements of her job were to get the room painted—presumably the construction company was going to do that—hire an artist to do a mural, order furniture and assemble some kind of play area. Three things. She could finish this. She took her notes from her first visit to the office furniture showroom and reviewed dimensions and compared it to the size of the room, drawing little Xs on the paper, becoming so involved with her work that she forgot to eat lunch. She went out to buy a soft pretzel from a vendor who was stationed outside the hospital mid-afternoon and resumed her work.

Before she knew it, Fred was standing outside the door of her office.

"Oh, is it that late already?" she asked.

"All work and no play...."

"Yes, I am being a dull girl. I didn't realize it was so late."

Fred looked over her shoulder at the sketches and the notes she had made. "Looks important. You'll be overseeing construction projects soon."

"Ha! I don't think so. Not if I would have to work with the likes of the men downstairs. All they seem to do is yell at one another or mope around."

"That's just how working men feel they must behave to get respect from the others. Can you imagine one of them saying, "Excuse me, Joe, would you please hand me the hammer? Thank you ever so much," he said in a polite singsong.

She laughed at his impersonation.

"No, they say, 'Hey, Joe. Gimme the hammer!'"

Amanda stood up and eased the tightness in her shoulders. "I guess I'll just have to toughen up and learn a new way of speaking. Hey, Fred, gimme my coat!" she tried out to get him to laugh.

He helped her into her coat, and she realized that talking to Fred was easy and he was a comforting presence. She couldn't imagine them ever having an argument about anything, not politics, food or friends. That should be the basis of a solid relationship.

Fred put his hands on her shoulders and asked in a quiet voice, "When were you going to tell me that you were seeing someone else?"

Amanda was too quick in her answer, "I'm not." Then she amended it. "If you mean the person I was with at the club, which I'm sure Caroline told you, it was that detective. I asked him to go with me to check out the Oasis to make sure it was a legitimate place for Louisa to be spending her time."

His hands returned to his side. "And?"

"He looked around the building, even inspecting the basement, and didn't find anything illegal. But I still don't approve of her seeing Rob Worley and going to his club."

"But it's all right for you to go. And then on to a speakeasy?"

"Yes, just as your sister did."

"That's different."

"How is it different? I don't like the tone of this conversation," Amanda said.

"Neither do I."

There were some moments of silence before she said, "I think we had better call off dinner tonight." She reached over his shoulder to turn off the light and brushed past him to the elevator. It was a wordless trip.

It was dark when they went outside to the nearly empty parking lot, not that there were ever many cars there since most people took the bus or the T to get to the hospital. The job site at the clinic was quiet and dark until the sound of a truck pulling up to the shed beside it with the headlights turned off.

Amanda and Fred looked at each other and stopped walking, wondering what deliveries could possibly take place so late in the day. The engine shut off and two men got out of the truck and went to the shed, the door to which was hidden from view by the truck itself.

"What do you think they're doing?" she asked.

"Let's see."

Despite their best efforts to get a glimpse of the activity, the looming truck didn't allow a clear line of sight and when Amanda started forward, Fred held her back.

"We'll just watch."

Amanda bent down and could just make out the feet of the men between the bottom of the truck and the road.

"They're taking out a dolly of some kind," she said. "And pulling down a ramp." Fred bent down beside her to look.

The two men silently went back and forth between the shed and the truck and then their movement stopped, and the back doors of the truck were closed with a bang. The driver got in the truck, started the engine without the head-lights coming on, and the other man got in the passenger seat. Instead of driving toward Amanda and Fred, the truck backed out into the road behind the hospital before turning on its lights and driving away.

They waited until they could see the truck out of sight before approaching the shed.

"It's locked," Fred said, pulling on the sizable lock that was slung between the metal rings, one attached to the door, the other to the wall. "What in the world?"

"We ought to call the police," Amanda said.

"Your friend the detective?"

"Fine. I'll wait until I get home to call the police. There's nothing they can do about it now since we didn't see their faces or the license plate." She strode to his car and waited for him to unlock the door.

Nothing was said on the drive to Beacon Hill until they got to her front door.

"I'm sorry if I overstepped…," Fred began.

Not waiting for him to open the passenger door, Amanda merely said, "Goodnight. Thank you for the ride home."

Once inside, Amanda went to the telephone and called the police station and asked for Detective Halloran.

"Are you checking up on me?" he asked.

"I don't need to. You always seem to be at work. Well, most of the time. I'm calling because of an unusual situation we witnessed on the hospital grounds just a little while ago."

"We?"

"Fred Browne and I were leaving the building and saw what looked like a burglary. A break-in of the construction company's shed behind the clinic." She went into some detail about what they had witnessed.

"Why didn't you go back into the hospital and call from there? We could have got there sooner than from this phone call."

"We didn't see their faces or the license plate and when we checked the shed, it was locked up.

"Then that doesn't sound like a break-in if somebody had a key."

"Oh. I hadn't thought of that. But why would somebody be out in the dark taking things?"

"Maybe someone working late. It sounds strange, but I can't see looking into it at this hour. I'll contact the construction company and take a look tomorrow. I'm glad you didn't put yourself in danger. And thank you for the call." He hung up.

Chapter 18

Halloran was out at the site as the sun was coming up about the same time as the workmen straggled into the empty building looking at him warily. The foreman burst out of the clinic building and confronted the detective.

"What do you want?"

Halloran opened his overcoat to show him his badge. "Who might you be?"

"Greco. Tony Greco," he replied. Shorter than Halloran, he was broader in the shoulders and chest and was standing an inch closer than he should, his dark eyes drilling into the detective's.

"Nice to meet you." Halloran put out his hand obliging the other man to shake it.

"What's going on?"

"Someone reported a break-in here last night."

Greco's eyebrows pulled together. "What? Everything's okay inside," he gestured back to the clinic building. "There's not much to take in there except my heater and the generator and they're both still here."

"No, the shed here."

Greco leaned his head around Halloran's body and looked. "It's locked." Nonetheless, he walked over to it and jiggled the lock to make sure.

"Do you have a key?"

"Yeah." Greco went back into the clinic and returned with a key and fit it into the lock. The shed had no light but once the door was open there was enough daylight to see inside. The two men stepped inside and looked around at a largely bare space.

"Looks pretty empty. Did someone take your tools or equipment?"

"Nah. I keep my tools in my truck. Same with the other guys who bring their own. Nothing is missing."

Halloran noticed a wooden crate and a crowbar in one corner and scuffed dirt under his feet. "What do you store in here?"

"Me, nothing. My boss put in the shed for when some of the materials get here. You know, paint and such as we don't need right away. When we get the lumber, we'll lock it in the building. The boards are too big to fit in here." He stepped back out and Halloran followed.

"Do you keep the key in a secure place?"

"Sure. It's in my desk inside."

"So, anyone could use it?"

Greco was silent a moment. "I guess. But there's nothing in there."

"Yes, I saw," Halloran said. He nodded his head and walked across the parking lot. Amanda was pulling her car into a spot, and he flagged her down. She rolled down the window.

"And?" she asked.

"Nothing but something's fishy. Are you going inside?"

She nodded, turned off the engine and got out.

"You're here early," he said.

"As are you. What did you find out?" She turned to look back in the direction of the clinic to see the foreman observing them.

"Niente," Halloran said with a slight smile, holding his hand up and shrugging.

"Well, I know what I saw. It was something."

"Perhaps."

He held the door to the hospital open for her and asked, "Is there a canteen or cafeteria here somewhere?"

"Yes, it's in the basement." She thought it was an odd question.

"May I treat you to a cup of coffee? Or something more? I haven't had breakfast yet."

They took the elevator down to the lower level and walked past men rolling baskets of sheets and towels through double doors that burst open with steam as they wheeled them into the laundry. Workmen passed them as Amanda and Halloran walked the length of the corridor and pushed through another set of double doors into a utilitarian cafeteria which she had only been in once before. Breakfast fare was available at this early hour: scrambled eggs, bacon, sausage, potatoes and pastries.

"I'll have a cinnamon roll, please," Amanda said, taking the plate offered by one of the women behind the counter and placing it on her tray.

"That's all?" Halloran asked.

"It will do."

He got the full breakfast and then coffee for them both, went to the cashier, paid and led them to a table away from others who might overhear. Amanda looked around her as they moved through the room to see if Fred might be among the early diners, but he was not there.

"What do you make of the foreman?" she asked.

"He's as dodgy as they come. I think it would be a good idea for me to keep watch on the shed this evening."

"Do you think something else will happen? I did notice on other occasions that one of the workmen would be stationed in front of the shed as if he were guarding it. Perhaps I was imagining it. And the foreman is often chastising the men, but he is speaking in Italian, and I can't understand what he is saying. However, the loud voice, the tone and poking a finger in the chest of the other man told me that he wasn't pleased with something."

"I'd like to talk to Mr. Barlow about my suspicions and see what station I could take up in this building to best observe what's going on out there."

"All very cloak and dagger," Amanda said.

"All very serious, I'm afraid."

He had embarrassed her into silence while she cut the cinnamon roll with a fork and knife and ate a piece.

"Do you always do that?"

"What? Cut up my food? Of course."

He smiled. "That's not usually how people eat those."

"It's how I do it," she said. "After you're done wolfing down your breakfast, I'll take you up to ask Mr. Barlow's permission for your—whatever you call it."

"Stakeout."

Amanda was beginning to feel she was in a gangster movie with all the terminology she had heard. No, that was silly. This was her city, the hospital where she volunteered and then worked. The foreman and his crew might be coarse, but they were not involved in anything illegal, surely. Not in full view of so many passersby and hospital staff.

Mr. Barlow had just come in when they approached, and Amanda introduced the detective and explained what she and Fred had seen the night before and why he was there that morning.

"Sit, sit," Barlow instructed. "What do you think is going on?"

"Naturally, Fred and I thought that someone was stealing something but then Detective Halloran interviewed the foreman." She let him take it from there.

"He opened the shed for me and there was nothing inside but a crate and a crowbar. He said nothing of theirs had been stored there and so nothing was stolen. But someone had been in there, based on the disturbance of the dirt. It's only a corrugated shed plopped on the bare ground, after all. I'm curious as to what that shed is being used for."

"What do you propose?"

"I'd like to be able to watch from one of the rooms in the hospital that overlooks the clinic. At night, of course. No one is going to be coming and going in the daylight."

"If you think it's important," Barlow said, looking at Amanda, wondering what her connection with him was. "The windows facing the clinic are mostly the surgical recovery ward, but there might be a side room or a private room not in use that could work. You'd have to ask the doctor in charge of that section for permission, of course."

"Certainly. Who would that be."

Amanda waited for the shoe to drop.

"Doctor Browne. Why don't you make the arrangements, Amanda?"

Chapter 19

"This is going to be interesting," Amanda muttered as she led Halloran to her office to hang her coat on the rack in the corner.

"How so?" he asked.

She looked at him as if he were dense. "His sister was the one who told him about us being at the club together and he thinks there is something going on."

"Such as?"

"He asked if I were 'seeing someone else.' What does that tell you?"

"It tells me that he has great affection for you and is jealous. Why didn't you tell him before we went that we were going to the club to check up on Worley and Louisa?"

She took a deep breath and tried to review her decision-making process at the time. "Because he would have disapproved. And after hearing about it, he did."

"What has your going to a club—"

"And a speak-easy, thank you for that tidbit, Caroline—."

"Have to do with him? Is he a teetotaler?"

"No, I've seen him have a sherry."

"Well, well, then," Halloran said with a smile.

"What I mean is that he didn't think it appropriate behavior."

"For a woman? For you? You're not engaged, are you?" he asked.

"No, not engaged. But we have been seeing one another. I think that he has a strict vision of how women should behave."

"That's strange, if you don't mind me saying so. Should you behave like his sister? That would surprise him. How about his mother? I've heard enough tales about her. And the older brother, now in prison."

"Perhaps Fred is trying to amend the family's reputation. I don't know."

"That's well and good, but what about you? Do you have to fit into his mold? What if you wanted him to fit into yours?" He tilted his head awaiting her answer.

"What an awful term—mold. Every time I hear it, I think of black fungus, or a type of thing you make in art class using a rubber form in which you pour the plaster. Either definition is terrible. That's not how people should look at one another: as if they have to fit a pattern that has been pre-determined. Oh, I don't know what I'm going on about. Maybe he doesn't think that way at all."

"I'll explain to him what we were up to. Perhaps that will ease his mind. But, first, let's locate him so I can set up the reconnaissance."

They went down to the surgical floor and asked where Doctor Browne might be and were told he was writing up some notes in his office, a room halfway down the hall where the door was closed. She knocked and he came to the door and opened it with surprise. Then his eyes fell on Halloran.

"Fred, you remember Detective Halloran," she began. She watched as they shook hands.

"I've got to go back upstairs, but you two can chat," she continued, smiled and walked away.

"Come into my palatial office," Fred gestured to the small desk, chair and another chair on which sat a stack of papers that he picked up and looked to move somewhere else although there was little other space for them.

"Don't bother. I'm here on two accounts. Amanda told me about what you had witnessed last night, and I am interested in observing the clinic from a window that faces in that direction. I figure from a certain height, such as this floor, I can have an excellent view."

"Now?"

"This evening. If anything suspicious happens, it will be when it's dark."

"I think I know of such a location. Would you like to see it?" Fred ushered Halloran back out into the hallway and led the way to one of the wings. "The room is basically used for storage, but it does have a window. You can't be wandering around the patients' rooms, you know."

"Understood. I'd like to come back about four o'clock and just station myself here with a pair of binoculars for the night."

"Really?"

"Yes, that's the sort of work it takes, unfortunately. Thank you, this will do fine."

Fred turned to leave.

"The other thing I wanted to say was that I went to a club at Amanda's request because she was worried about her younger sister and the company she had been keeping. She wanted me to evaluate the situation, the people and so on."

"And do you need to wear club clothes to do that?"

Halloran gave a short laugh. "It would have looked very strange if I were to go in uniform or even plainclothes street wear. We were trying to blend in." Now he knew that Caroline had given her brother a detailed account of what he and Amanda had been wearing. And probably the champagne. That sibling relationship must be complicated, he thought.

"No need to explain anything to me," Fred said, and without expression shook Halloran's hand and went back to his work.

Halloran went back to the station to retrieve binoculars and intended to get some paperwork done and possibly a bite to eat before returning to the hospital. He started to decipher the minute handwriting of the newest recruit's report when he sensed a figure looming in the doorway.

"Good afternoon, boyo. Getting ready for another evening on the town?"

Halloran stood up but the Chief motioned him to sit back down.

"No, sir, that was a one-off."

"Beautiful girl, that."

"Yes, I would have to agree with you."

"You don't *have* to agree with me."

"I believe it's wisest if I do."

The Chief let out a guffaw. "Don't we have a way with words?" He stepped forward and picked up a fountain pen that lay on Halloran's desk. "Are you still dogging that bootlegging gang?"

"Trying to, but the leads are few and they seem to be a step ahead all the time."

"Well, they've got the money and manpower and we only have you."

"If you assigned someone else to assist me, we might be able to go further with it."

The Chief tapped the pen on the desk and twisted his mouth to one side. "Let's see how things go in the next few months. There's a feeling that Prohibition is going to end sooner rather than later and then we'll have spun our wheels to no effect."

"Chief!" one of the secretaries said in the hall having spotted him in Halloran's office. "Your wife is on the phone."

"Now you know who's the boss in our household," the Chief said with a smile and followed the secretary back to his own office.

There was time for Halloran to finish up and grab a sandwich from the vendor down the street before going to the hospital although he supposed the hospital canteen might be open twenty-four hours a day for the doctors and nurses on night duty. He was about to get up when Gleason, the reporter, rushed up to his door and simultaneously rapped on the jamb and swept in, his coat flapping open.

"What's going on with the Harris murder investigation?"

"Would you like to sit down?"

"What I'd like is to get a decent night's sleep."

"Can't help you with that," Halloran said.

"No kidding. Got a two-month-old baby at home who doesn't seem to know the meaning of the term, either."

"We found the hobo who was on the scene shortly after Harris was shot. He said he saw a man—no further description—and rescued the dog that was wandering around. The end."

"That guy King is aptly named, or at least he thinks so. Lording it over the folks in the Buildings Department, or so I've heard."

"You hear a lot," Halloran said.

"Yes, but not the stuff I need. You talked to the widow, right? Did she give you any information?"

"Nothing that could be of use. She's a housewife living in a nice home who now has no financial support. Whatever Harris was or did at work, he didn't bring it home and share with her." He shrugged.

"It couldn't have been a robbery; the money and his watch were still on him."

"I see you've been talking to the coroner's staff. It could have been an attempted robbery that was interrupted by the distraction of the barking dog or the appearance of the hobo. That could explain why there was no time to hide the body. Somebody with a revenge motive would be more likely to try to cover up what he had done."

"Or she."

A pause.

"What do you know that I don't know?" Halloran asked.

"It wasn't the happiest of marriages."

"You wouldn't know it by the widow's reaction."

"That's to be expected."

"Do you suspect her of killing her husband? Where would she get a gun? How could the witness have mistaken her for a man?"

"I didn't say she actually did it. I heard he had a girlfriend on the side. Maybe she did it."

"Do you have a name?"

"Not yet. But either the wife or the girlfriend could have hired somebody."

Halloran looked at Gleason with disdain.

"You may think you deal with the criminal element, but brother, you don't know what regular folks are up to," Gleason said getting up.

"Let me know if you find anything else," Halloran said.

"It's a two-way street."

"Sorry to say, not really."

After the reporter left, Halloran looked at his watch. Although he didn't have a window to the outside, he knew by the time that it was starting to get dark. He put his pen away and shuffled the papers into a pile and knew that he was not looking forward to sitting in a little room for hours. Just as he stood up the recruit whose minute handwriting had given him a bit of headache poked his head around the corner.

"Sir, you wanted to see me?"

Up until that moment he was the last person he wanted to see until a rescue plan suddenly came to him.

"I hope you are free this evening," Halloran said with a serious look on his face.

"Yes, sir." The recruit was twenty but sometimes he seemed as if he were fourteen years old and eager to please.

"There's a stakeout that I need you to take on tonight."

"Really?"

Halloran maintained his stern demeanor but inside was relieved that he had found a more than willing volunteer. "Now, let me tell you what it is you're going to do."

Chapter 20

The family was assembled in the sitting room, a fire adding more atmosphere than heat with Mrs. Burnside toiling at some needlepoint, her husband engrossed in the newspaper and their two daughters each nursing a glass of sherry. Amanda was surprised to see that Louisa was at home for dinner and had no plans to sneak out to the club.

"Do you have a lot of studying to do?" she teased her sister.

"Not too much. I'm doing quite well."

"I had expected nothing less," said their mother. Amanda arched her eyebrows as she glanced at her sister.

"I don't think I told you that in working with Mr. Barlow, we've come to the conclusion that having people come from all over the city for the clinic is a real hardship for them so we're looking into additional sites where doctors and nurses could be available on some days a week."

"Like a circuit judge," her father commented, not looking up from his newspaper.

"Yes, that's the idea. Based on your experience, what neighborhood would you say might be most in need?" Amanda asked.

Her sister's eyes were wide as she searched for an answer. "That's a hard question. There are so many."

"You might find this funny, Daddy, but I chanced to meet the Mayor and when he heard of the idea, he was ready to jump on the wagon."

"I'm not surprised. The best way to get votes is to give your constituents something for free." He put the paper down to make eye contact with Amanda over the rim of his reading glasses. "My guess is he would choose the North End. He's already got the Irish vote and he needs to bolster the Democratic bloc among the Italians."

"I hadn't thought of it politically, but in terms of need, yes, the North End would be an excellent place for an additional clinic," Louisa said.

"How would it work, exactly?" her father asked.

"I'm not sure. But there must be someplace, like a church with a meeting room that isn't used all the time. Interns and residents could get some valuable experience working in a setting like that. Public health nurses, too," Amanda said.

"You could have other services, too. Like social workers, dentists, I don't know," Louisa added.

"We could be quite a team," Amanda said, not quite believing her sister was remotely interested in the idea.

"I know it is a colorful part of the city, but I'd be worried about your safety," their mother said.

"Nowhere is particularly safe. Think about someone trying to break into the house next door! Things can happen anywhere. And the work that I might do will not involve wandering around at night. I'll be finding the space, coordinating with the hospital and the main clinic and perhaps popping in from time to time to see how things are going."

Nora came in and announced that dinner was ready. Mrs. Burnside put her needlework back into its bag and gave her husband a concerned look. Her daughters' lives were turning out to be nothing like her own had been.

AMANDA GOT to the hospital early the next morning and thought to check on Halloran's surveillance activity, but when she opened the door to the storage room, she was surprised to see a young man seated with his head on his arms on the window sill, fast asleep. At the sound of her footsteps, he lurched awake.

"Who are you? They asked each other simultaneously.

"I'm a friend of Detective Halloran's and was one of the people who witnessed the suspicious activity in the first place that led to this stakeout."

"He asked me to take his place last night. I'm Officer O'Brien. Please don't tell him that I was asleep when you came in."

"My lips are sealed. Well, did you see anything of interest?"

"Nothing at all. Although I probably shouldn't be sharing that information with you."

"Again, I'll say nothing. I don't know if you're off duty yet, but there is a canteen downstairs in the basement where you could get a hearty breakfast. I'm sure the detective wouldn't think of you working twenty-four hours straight."

"And why not?" Halloran said, coming through the doorway. "In my day, that's how we started out. Trying like the devil to impress the boss."

"What day was that? You make it sound like you've been doing this for twenty years."

"If I were, I'd be retired with a nice police pension and looking for something else to do. No, I've only been there six years."

O'Brien, for one, was impressed. "Would you mind if I got something to eat?"

"What's your report?"

"I haven't written it up yet, but according to my notes, there was no activity at the building or the shed. Just one or two cars coming into the parking lot with people entering the hospital. All quiet."

"Good. Dismissed. Have your meal and take the rest of the day off."

"Thank you, sir," he said, his young face beaming and he hurried to the elevator.

"Whatever is going on out there might not happen for several nights yet," Halloran said.

"What do you think is going on?"

"I think someone is using that shed to store something before moving it to another location. Something that they don't want the police to know they've got."

They walked into the hallway.

"Who is the 'they' you're looking for?" Amanda asked.

"I'm pretty sure it's bootleggers. Despite all the nonsense that Worley was trying to feed us the other night about Detroit being the center of trade, we well know that the port of Boston is where a lot of it comes in. With so many boats and ships and points of access, it's perfect. Although my boss doesn't really think it's worth putting any effort into."

"Why not?" Amanda asked.

Halloran looked around to see if anyone was in hearing distance. "Lazy would be the kindest answer." He put his finger to the side of his nose.

"Do you think...?"

"I try not to think about it. I'm doing my job as best I can with all kinds of distractions being thrown in my face. Gleason showed up yesterday with a wild theory that either the wife, the girlfriend or a hitman killed Harris."

"Hitman?" Amanda whispered as they approached the elevators. She pushed the button to go up assuming that he might follow and elaborate. A nurse got in as the doors opened, which did not afford the opportunity for further discussion until they exited at the tenth floor.

"Hitman?" Amanda repeated. "Where does one hire a hitman?"

"Why, are you looking for someone to rub out?" he asked with a smile.

"Not at the moment. But how would someone like Mrs. Harris, who appears to be a regular housewife, know where to hire a hitman?"

"I think that theory is highly unlikely. As for the girlfriend insinuation, that seems to have been circulated by Mr. King, who has done his best to discredit his former boss."

The doors opened and Amanda greeted Miss Bailey and took Halloran to her office. "Luxurious, wouldn't you say?" she asked as she removed her coat and put it on the rack by the door. "Please, make yourself at home," she said, noting that he still had his hat and coat on.

"Thank you," he said, sitting in the chair adjacent to her small desk. After a moment he said, "Another interesting thing occurred this morning. Miss Jones from the Buildings Department came to see me and was very nervous about the visit. She was the one who ushered the paperwork through the approval process and said that King was notoriously slow in processing the applications because she had heard him chew Harris out about it more than once. She also said that Harris' office was usually neat as a pin while King's was the one with paperwork scattered about. She had been in Harris' office Friday after he left for the day and those files were not there."

"What do you think happened?"

"I think once he realized Harris was dead——"

"Or killed him?"

"Over sloppy paperwork? Probably not. But to save his bacon King hastily signed off on all the pending paperwork with a date a week or two before, nicely scattered along each day of the week. While cleaning up the mess of paperwork that was left in Harris' office afterward, Miss Jones noticed that the date on one of the applications was wrong."

"In what way?"

"You would assume that King had done his duty, signed off and forwarded it to Harris, who let it sit in a folder on a shelf. Once King became Director, he had the job of doing the final sign-off, so his name now actually appears twice on those documents. That's fine. But on one application King inadvertently put the date when he wasn't even in the office. The application for the clinic."

"How do you know that?"

"The secretary took all the approvals down to be recorded and she noticed that the one application was missing from the pile. She went back up to her desk thinking she must have dropped or misplaced it, then went to King's office where she saw it on his wastebasket, ripped in half."

"He made an error and tried to cover it up?" Amanda asked.

"Yes, and then reinitiated the paperwork and re-signed the documents and gave them to his secretary the next day, saying it must have slipped onto the floor."

"That must have been the same day that he insisted on bringing the completed paperwork to Mr. Barlow with much fanfare. So, he's a liar and schemer. But do you think he killed his boss?"

"I'm not sure, but I told the secretary to be very careful, perhaps stay home from work."

Amanda's eyes widened. "I hope she doesn't live alone. She'd be safer at work with other people around."

"No, I asked. Big family. She'll be okay."

"But Brendan, if Ron King didn't kill his boss over sloppy administration, who shot him? And why?"

"I think Patrick Harris knew something else that was dangerous. There is clearly something I'm missing. I've got to go back to the station, but I'll return this afternoon for my round of surveillance."

Chapter 21

It was difficult for Amanda to concentrate on her work that day with the image of Ron King's phony heartiness toward her which could mask some seriously nasty intentions. Her quiet morning was interrupted by a call from the Mayor, who said he had some information on possible locations for expansion sites for the clinic. Rather than go into detail, he suggested that she call his secretary and set up a meeting with an aide to whom he had assigned the project. It came at her so fast that all she could say was thank you before feeling like an idiot for not saying something more. What that would have been, she couldn't think, but surely one of his cronies would go on about what a great man he was and promise a favor in return.

She promptly reported the conversation to Mr. Barlow who was just as surprised as she at how quickly things were moving. After a hasty lunch in the canteen, she had appointments with two different furniture suppliers and went to the first showroom expecting to be in and out quickly. Despite having taken measurements of the clinic's reception room and the size of one of the existing chairs, she did not expect to be bombarded with so many questions.

"While we often recommend wood guest chairs for reception areas, seeing as this is in a hospital setting, you might be better off with metal frames. More hygienic," he added to her puzzled look.

"Would you prefer chairs with armrests?"

"That seems sensible as it would allow a woman with a baby to rest her arm while holding it," she said but then the salesman shook his head.

"If there are armrests, the chairs are not stackable."

"Is that so important?"

"In the event the room is needed for some other use, it is imperative. And the janitors will need to be able to move them easily to clean the floor. Let's talk about capacity."

The interrogation went on to include the dimension of the tubes, the color, the method of cleansing and whether she might prefer a few benches as well.

"What about the fabric?" she asked.

"No, no, no. We can't sell you fabric furniture for a hospital setting. *You know.*" He said in a tone that put her mind to thinking of lice, bedbugs and other creatures.

"Based on what we discussed, could you send me a bid for the number of chairs we need?"

She staggered out to her car, clutching the salesman's business card and brochure in her hand, congratulating herself on not having chosen interior design as a job. She still had two more appointments with other companies' representatives; however, she felt more informed about the intricacies of waiting room chairs and that meeting went more quickly.

It was already dark by the time she returned to the hospital and reported to Mr. Barlow about what she had done that day and that they could expect to be able to sort through the budget more carefully soon. She went to her office and put the brochures she had received into a file folder before putting on her coat. Taking the elevator down, curiosity got the better of her and she pushed the button for the surgical floor to see if Halloran was watching from the storage room.

The only sound on that floor was the clattering of staff wheeling partially eaten trays of food out of patients' rooms as the day was winding down. She tapped on the door, and he swung it inward, surprised to see her.

"Anything going on tonight?"

"Not yet. What you and Fred saw might have been a one-time event. I can tell you I'm not going to spend from now to eternity sitting here."

"I thought that's what recruits were for," she said.

"He's got to learn about shoe leather."

She looked puzzled.

"It usually means walking around, talking to people to get information just as reporters do. I guess sitting in a hard-backed chair is not quite the same."

"If you'll be here for a while I'll be back." She left and closed the door. She could hear him muttering about going nowhere.

An hour later, Amanda, still wearing her coat, returned with a bag and a thermos.

"What's that?" Halloran asked.

"Roast beef on rye with horseradish sauce. Care to have some?"

He jumped up and pulled another chair over toward the window. There was enough illumination from a streetlight to see inside the room without pulling the string to the bare bulb overhead and revealing their presence.

"I think you must be an angel," he said.

"Coffee with cream and sugar, too."

"Now I'm certain."

"I've made friends with someone on the canteen staff. This is not usually on the menu."

"Very good. Very, very good," he said. After that, they ate in silence while Halloran periodically looked through his binoculars.

"I think this project may be a dud."

Amanda put her sandwich down into a napkin in her lap, pulled something out of her pocket and put it up to her face.

"What are those?"

"Opera glasses, of course. Just the right size for surveillance."

"Now, wait a minute. I appreciate that you have brought me a meal, which I suspect was really a bribe, but you can't take part in this operation."

"Whyever not? I was the one who tipped you off—I think that's the expression. I'm the one who found you this blind from which to watch the action. I am already invested in this operation, as you put it. I'm staying right here until something happens. Or doesn't."

"It will be a long wait," he said. "And I don't think we should talk and alert anyone walking by in the hall that someone is in here."

"Mum's the word."

They sat in silence, each taking turns to see if there was anything of interest at the far end of the parking lot. Amanda looked at her watch and saw it was eight-thirty.

"I hate to be the one to say it, but I probably should be going home."

"That's a good idea. Your family might be worried sick."

"Actually, I think they have gotten used to my strange comings and goings and have been oblivious about what Louisa has been up to. Still, it's been a long day." She got up.

"Let me walk you to your car. As you have realized, there may be nefarious people about."

As they rode the elevator, Halloran asked, "Are things all right between you and Fred now?"

"I don't know. I haven't seen or spoken to him today." She looked over at him. "Why do you ask?"

"He seemed a bit stiff yesterday when we were talking and setting up this up."

Amanda smiled. "He can come off that way."

"I thought it in everyone's best interest to explain more fully why we were at the club."

"Whose interest? Don't you think I can fend for myself?"

The doors opened to the first floor, and she bolted out before he had a chance to respond, which was her intention.

"Hold up," he said. "I can hardly walk you to your car if you are sprinting ahead."

She stopped at the doors and allowed him to open them for her.

"Fred was right about one thing: I am independent."

"And possibly a little bit stubborn," he added.

They walked across the dark lot to where her car had been parked since that afternoon when many more cars were there and now, they could hear some clanking noise. Halloran grabbed her arm and pulled her closer to him.

"Shh. That may be them again."

They hunkered down and using what few cars were left as a shield, crept closer to the clinic and were able to get a clear view of the shed. The same kind of truck that Amanda had seen previously, one with no identifying markings on the side, was parked next to the shed. Now both she and Halloran could see a sturdy man with a fedora next to the open door of the shed and two others unlocking the back of the truck.

"Are they delivering or removing?" Amanda asked in a whisper.

"If they are delivering, we can leave knowing the evidence is there. Unless someone is coming later in the evening. If they are removing, it looks like O'Brien must have nodded off."

They crept a little closer, still well out of the line of sight of the men who were wheeling dollies down the ramp at the back of the truck and going into the shed and coming out with something significantly heavy. The sturdy man was no longer blocking their view and they could see that the loads consisted of boxes—of what? Now there was only one man working as they peeped out from behind the front bumper of a car, and they looked at each other questioning why the work had slowed down.

"Stand up slowly," said a voice behind them. "And don't turn around," he commanded.

"Put your hands up."

Halloran and Amanda obeyed and stood in that awkward position until they heard another set of footsteps come up and yank Amanda's arm down and propel her toward the shed. She tried to get a look at him, but he shoved her forward.

"Don't try anything, sister," he said. All she could make out was a snap brim cap over a brutal face some inches taller than she. Amanda could hear that Halloran was been pushed forward by the sturdy man and that he either was resisting or not moving fast enough.

When they got close to the open door of the shed, she was pushed inside the dark room and fell to the ground on her hands and knees with a yelp. Then she heard a thud and a groan, and Halloran's body was pushed into the shed after her. He landed nearby and didn't make a sound.

"Keep going," the man with the fedora said to the two workers who came back into the shed with a small flashlight and hefted the last two loads onto the dollies. He managed to keep his head down under the shade of his hat to avoid detection.

It became clear that they intended to leave Amanda and the detective locked inside and she got up and ran to the door in just enough time to see Ron King shove her back inside, fit the lock in the metal loop and click it shut.

"No, no! Let us out!" she yelled, pounding on the corrugated surface feeling the cold even through her gloves. She heard the engine start and the truck pulled away without turning on its headlights.

Amanda went to Halloran and felt for where his face was and patted him on the cheeks to revive him, but what if he had been killed by the blow to his skull? She reached down under his collar and felt for a pulse. Luckily there was one, so she undid his tie and the top button of his shirt, letting him at least breathe more easily. She sat back on her haunches and wondered what she could do. Someone would come in the morning, but that would be almost nine hours later. They could freeze to death in that time. She had no matches or lighter and there was no illumination in the shed; she couldn't even see what was in there with them.

Slowly, Amanda made her way to where she knew the door was, there being a slight chink of light where the door and wall did not meet. She knew that the shed was rectangular, and she moved along the wall, feeling her way, hoping to encounter something that could be of use.

"Damn," she said as she barked her shin on what felt like a crate. Of what? She felt its dimensions and could tell it was wooden although she had no implement of any kind to pry it open. Then she thought Halloran must have a weapon of some sort. If he had a gun, she wouldn't even try to use it, never having fired a handgun, only hunting rifles, and she knew they were entirely different things. She shuffled away from the crate, careful not to step on him and encountered the edge of his coat.

Kneeling, she felt for his pockets and encountered the handgun and quickly withdrew her hand. The other pocket of the coat held a handkerchief and what felt like a notebook. More boldly, she put her hands in the pockets of his suit jacket and could only detect a money clip and some change, the other pocket being empty. She leaned over his body and encountered something hard on his lower leg. Did he wear a brace of some sort? No, that wasn't possible. She hadn't noticed him limping earlier. She pulled up his pant leg and probed with her fingers in the dark and suddenly smiled.

A knife. He had a knife strapped to his leg!

She slid it out carefully and went back to the crate to find out if she could pry open one of the top boards. It was heavy going and she was afraid she would cut her hand in doing so, but finally was able to pull one slat back. Amanda felt inside the crate and encountered a bottle. Many bottles, in fact. She was cold enough by that time that she wished she had a corkscrew in order to open one of the bottles and take a long sip to get warm.

There was not much else to do but resume her slow walk edging around the room to feel what else was there. Scuffing her feet forward she hit something metal and bending down, traced the outline of a crowbar partly buried in the dirt. Salvation! How she was going to get them out of the shed with only a crowbar, she didn't know but she went back to the door and started jamming the pointed end at the place where she had seen the lock earlier. The metal on metal made a tremendous sound that echoed in the shed and she finally heard a moan from behind her.

"Brendan? Is that you?"

More moaning and then it stopped.

"Sorry, I'm trying to get us out of here." After several more minutes of bashing at the door, she was able to pry the metal of the door open a half inch and could see the outline of the lock. She swung it harder and harder and heard a voice on the other side.

"Is somebody in there?" it asked.

She froze. Had they come back? Should she be quiet or scream in the hopes that some passerby—as if there were any at this time of night—might hear her?

"I said, is somebody in there?"

Amanda waited. "I'm locked in here. Who are you?"

"I'll get help," it said, and she heard the somebody running away.

"No, no! Come back!"

Silence.

Amanda dropped the crowbar, her arms burning from the earlier exertion and slumped onto the ground. The cold, the fear and now the frustration of being found and abandoned were too much for her and not holding back any longer, she began to cry.

"Don't be sad. I'm not dead. Yet," Halloran said. By the sound of his voice, he was no longer lying on the ground but had managed to prop his upper body up. "Where are we?"

"We're in that miserable shed. Don't you remember?"

He groaned. "My head...."

"Yes, Ron King whacked you on the back of the head. I guess we're lucky he didn't shoot us instead."

They heard noises outside and Amanda got up and put her mouth to the opening in the door. "Help! We're in here!" she said, then put her eye to the space to see who or what was there.

"Don't worry. Hold on. We have to get some tools to break the lock. Stay right there," a man's voice said.

"Don't leave!" Amanda pleaded.

"I'll stay until he gets back," the voice from earlier said.

"Who are you?"

"Edwin Crouse. I was passing by and heard the noise. I got someone from the hospital. They'll get you out in no time."

"I know that name," Halloran said. "He's the hobo with the dog from the Common."

Chapter 22

Halloran and Amanda were taken into the hospital and Fred dashed to her side, taking in the ripped stockings, scraped knees, broken fingernails and filthy clothes in one long glance.

"Oh, my dear! What have you been doing?"

"A voice from the other side of the curtain asked, "Aren't you worried about me, Doctor Browne? I'm the one who got hit on the head."

Fred pulled the curtain that separated the two beds in the emergency room and saw Detective Halloran trying to look pathetic but still with a smile on his face.

"Head injuries can be dangerous. Let me see," Fred said, palpating the back of the other man's head. "Solid as a rock. But still, you might want to spend the night here."

"And what about me? A perfectly good pair of hose ruined."

"You're lucky that's all that happened. Let me find a nurse to help," Fred said, walking away and calling out to someone.

"Well, we know Ron King is part of the bootlegging operation. I'm guessing that Harris somehow found out and that's why he shot him," Amanda said to Halloran.

"We'll never get proof that King shot his boss. Since you can identify him, he'll have to plead to kidnapping or assaulting a police officer. He won't sing about the liquor business, that's for sure."

"What? Now he's left two families bereft. Harris' wife and his own if he is sent to prison."

"Which will certainly happen. I wouldn't worry about his own family, though. If he keeps his mouth shut, then while he is away, someone will pay the mortgage, the Catholic school tuition and probably the First Communion outfits for the kids. That's the price he'll pay for his silence."

Amanda sighed. "In any case, we made a pretty good team back there."

Halloran rose onto his elbow. "Don't get any ideas. You'll go back to Beacon Hill and get scolded for your antics tonight and be back in your office tomorrow. I'm the one who has to go back to the station and explain what you were doing with me and how the bootleggers got away with the booze."

"Not entirely. They took away all but one crate's worth. It's still in the shed."

He looked at her for a moment. "When they let us out of here, I think we need to make a trip to that blasted shed and we can take a bottle each after putting the rest of it in evidence."

"Fifty-fifty?" she asked.

"Sure."

"Like partners?"

"As I said before, don't get any ideas."

Is Amanda thinking she can assist Halloran in other cases?
Of course! Will he allow her?
That is another story.

MURDER IN BOSTON'S NORTH END

Check out my website for more titles.
www.Andreas-books.com
If you enjoyed this book, please let other readers know.
Reviews help readers discover my books, so feel free to leave a short line or two on

MY REVIEW SITE

SEE ALL THE BOOKS

Thank you! Happy Reading,
Andrea